Renascence

LEIGH GOODISON

SHEFFIELD PUBLICATIONS

The text for this book was set in Garamond.

Printed and bound in the United States of America.

10 9 8 7 6 5 4 3 2

Leigh Goodison

Renascence / Leigh Goodison / 1st edition

Summary:
Six young scientists are sent to colonize an exoplanet
only to discover that the Russians got there over a century earlier.

[1. Apocalyptic & Post-apocalyptic-Fic. 2. Space Exploration-Fic.]

I. Title

ISBN-13: 978-1-945136-12-2

Cover design and Copyright: SelfPubBookCovers.com/tgresh

DEDICATION

This book is dedicated to the notion of world peace,
though not through a one world order as indicated
in the formation of the fictional
Order of World Leaders.

"I saw and heard and knew at last
The How and Why of all things, past,
And present, and forevermore.
The Universe, cleft to the core."

From "Renascence," a poem by
Edna St. Vincent Millay
(1892–1950)

Renascence

LEIGH GOODISON

AUTHOR'S NOTE

The first draft of *Renascence* was created in November 2011. Because of commitments with other projects, it sat on a backburner until late 2016. The original premise was a reverse Big Bang theory: a cataclysmic event that had earth deteriorating at an accelerated rate. Ultimately, I didn't have to manipulate the plot line because when doing research, I discovered that life on earth really is deteriorating at a rate far beyond our imagination. Which is how the subplot on earth's future insufficiency of phosphorous evolved.

Like most science fiction novels, speculation and a certain amount of license has been taken regarding scientific facts and possibilities though what is impossible today might be tomorrow's technology.

I'd long been fascinated with the notion of the Lost Cosmonauts, the unverified and undocumented Russian astronauts of the Soviet Space Program from the late 1950s to early 1960s. Many of the details of the space race between the United States and Russia is cloaked in secrecy, thus their mission, portrayed in this book, is completely fictional.

I

The courier, a solemn-faced boy of about thirteen rotations, brought the orders to my compartment shortly before commencement of morning instruction. He flinched when I opened the door, as people seeing me for the first time often do, and I'd come to expect it. He wore the burgundy page's tunic with the OWL insignia, which caused my heart rate to quicken for I knew he came on official business. I accepted the folder without comment, nodding my thanks as he gave a slight bow of acknowledgement.

Through my tiny porthole window I watched him leave, staring out at a twister that sprang up in his wake. Then another followed, and another, until the entire sky was filled with whirlpooling dust, peppering my window against a landscape that could never be green again.

Once he'd gone I snapped the wax seal on the slender folder. As I removed the document my hands trembled like those of an old woman, though I couldn't have said why. Then as I read the letter I realized that the moment I'd been anticipating had finally arrived.

While I contemplated the contents and the ramifications, my stationary communicator buzzed and the face of my best friend, Rho, appeared on the monitor. Leaning back in the convertible chair-sleeper I pressed the button that allowed two-way communication. While it sprang to life I took a sip of the half-finished flask of liquid breakfast nutrients, an unappetizing greenish-brown blend of kale, brown rice, and vitamins, and force-swallowed it.

"A courier served me with orders from the OWL," she said. "I don't know what to do." Her hazel eyes glistened with either apprehension or fear. Hard to tell from what little detail of her I could make out through the monitor.

"Nothing for you to do," I replied. "I received the same orders."

She waited for me to say something more, reassure her perhaps, but as I possessed no more information than she, I remained silent for a few more moments. My thoughts drifted to my boyfriend, Lucian. By now, he should have received his orders. Though we'd secretly been pledged to each other for only two moons, during the brief opportunities we had to be together it seemed as if no one else in the world existed.

"We'll be debriefed." I finally responded. "And there will be training. A lot of it. No need to worry yet." But I'd formulated my words only to make her feel better, because even I had no idea what our fate would be now. We'd know within the next six moons.

In the days following the global announcement that earth's natural resources were nearly depleted, and after the ensuing panic and rioting subsided, there existed a poisonous calm. It was 2072 and the Order of World Leaders, or the OWL as they were generally referred to, assured our people what only a handful of us already knew: that for many rotations scientists had been working on finding a habitable exoplanet and were nearing a breakthrough. That part was true.

Before the creation of the OWL, unscrupulous politicians capitalized on fear and greed, pitting citizens against each other by rationing food and supplies to those who served their own interests. People wealthier than others lived in fear as the lawful and lawless alike struggled to feed themselves and their families, and the streets ran crimson with the blood of the hungry and needful.

To control the panic, warring nations set off a series of preemptive strikes, warning encroaching insurgents away by detonating nuclear bombs, all but decimating their population and that of those around them. Radiation, pollution, lack of water conservation, and ultimately the inability to grow crops, rendered the planet a wasteland. The population was forced to turn vegetarian as it was more efficient to use the precious fertilizer and energy resources to grow crops, rather than meat. As I'd never tasted meat, the notion of consuming the flesh of animals was as abhorrent to me as the thought of eating another human.

With much of the technology gained over the past two centuries destroyed, out of necessity, human ingenuity surged. Outside the cities, collective farms and communes were created to raise crops for feeding the population. While the fear of starvation kept the people working for the greater good of everyone, a grudging contentment and less consumption appeared to be the only victory.

We'd all known from our earliest education that sustaining life on our fragile planet would come at a cost, so the OWL's revelation couldn't have arrived at a better time. Having burned through all the fossil fuels decades before I was born, we'd converted to hydrogen as a virtually unlimited fuel supply for thirsty vehicles and heating our homes. We finally began to conserve, but even when housing compounds were constructed within the cities to reduce sprawl, it came too late. And as the air became less breathable outside, most citizens turned to wearing oxygen masks everywhere they traveled.

But all things must come to an end. Under strict rationing, the food and clean water supply was said to be sufficient to last no more than three rotations, or years, as they used to be called. We needed fresh air to breathe, and we could not live without water or food. Without these all ten billion life forms on earth would eventually extinguish in a series of choking, gasping breaths.

Having reached the age of eighteen rotations, I would be one of six recruited scientists trained and sent out in an exploration ship, the Astraeus, to locate an uninhabited exoplanet with the highest ESI, or Earth Simulation Index, and life sustaining resources. Once we recruits established an operations base, future expeditions would be sent out, and ultimately the remaining population of earth would be relocated.

The scout teams were staffed with nothing more than drones produced by generations of military families, or children raised as orphans when their own families died. Before the formation of the OWL, the practice was denounced as being in violation of human rights. But in reality it was no different than the age-old tradition of a first-born Catholic son considered to be destined for priesthood. Our objective was to save humanity, not souls. Never a light burden.

My soul still ached from my last conversation with Lucian. After learning Rho would be on the mission, lightheaded with excitement I buzzed Lucian's communicator to share our news and to make plans for our departure together.

"Has the courier from the OWL brought your folder yet?" I teased, certain he would have it by now. "Rho and I were chosen."

Lucian remained quiet for so long that it frightened me. As his russet complexion reddened to a deep umber, his head dropped, and he let his long black hair fall over his eyes to hide their expression.

"Yes," he said, his voice scarcely audible. "I received a folder."

"And?" I persisted. "You're coming with us, right?"

He cleared his throat and what sounded almost like a sob emerged. "I won't be with you," he said. "The medics discovered a previously undiagnosed heart defect. They decided that such a long and difficult journey could be fatal. Though my skills surpassed most of the other candidates', a health problem is an immediate rejection."

If his heart was damaged, mine felt as if it were ripped from my chest. His disappointment and shame for something beyond his control bled through the monitor to me. I found myself unable to speak, or even share with him how devastated I felt.

"You know I won't be able to communicate with you while I'm out there," I murmured. "No one knows about us yet and we'll only be authorized to use the transmission equipment for speaking to the Command Unit Base."

He gave me a sad smile. "I'll have you with me here in my heart," he said. "Complete the mission and promise me you'll come home safe."

"I promise," I whispered. "We'll have a lifetime together once I return."

The final team appointed by the OWL, the "Wise Ones," as we nicknamed them, would be led by the legendary Captain Ralph Reynard, a retired former United States Marine from back when the United States still existed. We'd all heard stories of his previous campaigns and 'failure' was not in his vocabulary. Nor was failure even considered a possibility. Without air and water, and the ability to grow food, there could be no future. No life. And so a great responsibility fell on us all.

We called ourselves the "Chosen Ones," our team that consisted of six recruits and one leader. Three males; three females. And Captain Reynard. It was unspoken, though understood, that the logic behind a team balanced evenly between the sexes, and the relatively young age of the members, was for population 'restocking' purposes should the mission fail. And to that end, in addition to the barrage of medical exams, we'd been subjected to fertility and genetic testing as well. Medical histories exposed to scrutiny. Not an anomaly among us.

We weren't the first to be selected for such a mission. There had been many more in the past that hadn't been successful. Our team was smaller than those that embarked on earlier quests. This was partly due to the lack of fuel, but also because of the relatively compact size of the scout craft assigned to us to make the trip to a recently discovered exoplanet called Arianrhod.

Named for the Celtic goddess of fertility, rebirth and the weaving of cosmic time and fate, our target planet lay deep within the Triangulum Galaxy. More crew would take up valuable space, meaning less room to bring back samples from the local terrain, which would be stored in heat and leak protected tanks in case of radioactivity. Of course, fewer team members also meant less available labor to perform the work. There was always a trade-off.

Two days left until we were to blast off for Arianrhod, or Planet A, as the OWL called it. Though it was believed to be uninhabited, from what we'd been taught, its atmosphere had a high potential for sustaining some forms of life; which ones we weren't entirely sure. To that end, until we determined its ESI, we needed to wear specially equipped suits and helmets at all times when outside the ship, or court death.

Our specialized training and the fitness regime for the mission had lasted six moons. A great deal of our instruction involved an unprecedented level of skill-building in our respective scientific discipline. Not to mention cooperation and trust in our fellow recruits. Two days prior to take-off there would be no slacking on anyone's part. It didn't help our exhausted bodies to remember that Captain Reynard had once been a drill sergeant while in active duty with the United States Marine Corps, and I will hear his morning roar until my dying day.

"Get up, bitches, daylight's burning!"

He meant 'bitches' in a generic way: we knew it was not a derogatory term toward the females. That would not have been tolerated by the rules created by the OWL. All Reynard's underlings were 'bitches.' And so we started each morning with a high energy breakfast of tablets meant to fill our energy requirements, though not our stomachs. It was important not to have much in our intestines during the flight for obvious reasons. Fortunately, in the training sessions they spared us the graphic details of the consequences.

Our team, as I mentioned before, consisted of seven individuals. Though we all answered to the birth names given us, once we became a member of the team we were instructed to adopt a Greek letter of our choice as our new name. The letters were our signature, which we would in turn use to sign off on a task performed, or as evidence of where we'd been. A sophisticated form of tagging, now that I think about it.

The three females were Xi, Rho, and me, Zeta. The males were Sigma, Omega, and Chi, and of course, Captain Reynard, who was differentiated from the team with his given name and title. Sigma shortened his name to 'Sig,' but the rest of us took to our new monikers as if we'd had them all our lives.

Despite our youth, the team brought to the mission a wealth of talent: archaeology, biology, botany, communications, engineering, geology, and medicine, to list only a fraction of the collective training. From earliest memory I had been schooled in chemistry. As a young child this training had been in the form of baking and cooking, which in turn prepared me for understanding chemistry, the correct balance of compounds and the results of mixing them. And how a miscalculation or mismeasurement here or there could lead to catastrophic results. Of course the team would have loved my cooking skills, but the nutrition tablets we ate in place of a decent meal and covered everything our bodies required in the way of protein, fats, and starches, made them unnecessary.

One day left and our last debriefing before launch. The seven of us were to meet at the training compound where we would be taken under the utmost secrecy to the OWL Headquarters in Quadrant I.

As we stood waiting for Captain Reynard, who was busy conversing with Hastings, one of the officials who had trained us in the art of properly obtaining and cataloguing samples to bring back from our mission, Rho whispered to me, "Are you nervous?"

I was about to shrug off the question with nonchalance, because I really wasn't afraid, but I saw naked apprehension in her eyes. Rho and I grew up together in the same compound in Quadrant II. Quadrant II encapsulated the former Soviet Union, China, and all the European countries. I'd known Rho from my earliest cognitive memory, and we were as inseparable as sisters.

"A little, but I'll get over it once we land."

Omega caught my attention and gave me a wink, which I ignored. He'd arrived at our training center over a rotation ago from Quadrant III, formerly most of Central and South America, the only other Quadrant I'd never visited. With copper-toned skin, a wide somewhat flat nose, and large dark-lashed brown eyes, he was considered to be dangerously handsome by my contemporaries. But my interests lay more in my burgeoning career, not in a potential romantic interest.

Out of the corner of my peripheral vision I saw Xi and Sig holding hands. Chi saw them too, and nudged them hard until they let go of each other as if they'd received a shock of electrical current.

Reynard finished his conversation with Hastings and motioned us over. The trainer held out black cotton triangles for each of us, demonstrating how to tie them so they occluded our vision completely. Then we were shepherded onto a shuttle vehicle and instructed to remain blindfolded for the duration of the two-hour journey. An unfamiliar voice conversing with Reynard led me to believe that we were accompanied by at least one additional person. As the shuttle came to a stop we were led, still masked, into a building.

Once we were allowed to remove our masks, we could see that we were in a cement block enclosure, and judging from the chilled temperature, probably underground. The only people remaining to escort us were Hastings and Reynard. Perhaps I'd been mistaken about an additional man with us on the shuttle, and the voice had belonged to the driver or one of the recruits.

The trainer and Reynard led us through concrete corridors, so cold we could see our breath as we walked. Light from recessed eyeball fixtures flooded the hallways though there was nothing to see except each other. We marched on until we came to an enormous stainless steel door that opened like an eye blinking into the oval framework. Inside the room, four stern-faced individuals wearing sexless burgundy tunics with the embroidered gold OWL insignia sat around an immense steel table, waiting for us to approach.

After the last Great War of 2054, the rotation of my birth, earth's entire population was reduced to less than a hundred thousand. Though crippled by the destruction and devastation, a tremulous peace had been sworn in. Earth was quadritioned into four regions called Quadrants, and each Quadrant was represented by one OWL member. Two of the OWL shared the northern hemisphere and two shared the south. They consisted of two men and two women, chosen to be leaders not by the people in their own hemisphere but by those in their neighboring Quadrant, a practice purported to reduce the potential for invasion.

What was known about the OWL was highly confidential and limited to only those with a 'need to know.' What we'd been told is that they were the offspring of Generals, trained leaders accustomed to positions of authority and unafraid of using draconian measures to achieve end results. Rumors surrounded the mystery of their rise to power: were they instated to prevent further outbreaks of conflict, or because they'd instigated the wars to create a new world order? I'd heard elders grumble about the evils of the 'new times' in which we now lived, but as I'd never known our planet before the war, I couldn't have told you if the old ways were better then than under the current OWL regime.

Though none of the recruits had previously met any of the OWL, we had no idea if the same were true about Captain Reynard. Even so, it came as a bit of a surprise that when we entered the room Reynard shared a curt nod of acknowledgement with a short, swarthy bald man, whose name plate read Hermes. We deferred to Reynard's cue, and he in turn waited for them to begin.

An older woman with a head of gray hair cropped short in a boxy cut motioned us to the chairs. A name plate that sat in front of her on the table read Artemis. Like the recruits, in the interests of anonymity, the OWL also forfeited their given names upon entering their official positions, and assumed those of Greek Gods that implied power. Dutifully we sat; then we listened to what would become our mantra for the next few weeks.

Hermes spoke first.

"You seven have been chosen above all the others because of your personal strengths and skills, which have been apparent since you were young. From your training you have learned what is required of you during this mission. In the past, other teams have tried and failed, but now we are at a pivotal point. The survival of our people rides on your shoulders. If you succeed in your mission, and with the research and preparation you have received there is no reason to believe otherwise, the rewards can exceed your wildest dreams. This is to be not only your first mission, but also your last, for you will be allowed to retire at an unprecedented age and kept in prosperity to the end of your days."

We all could not help smiling to ourselves at that point and casting sly glances at each other. While we knew this would not be the easy task it appeared, and outsiders might resent our good fortune, in truth we had been training and working toward something like this since infancy. Retirement at the ages of eighteen or twenty-one was not unthinkable.

As if reading my mind, Rho nudged me and murmured, "As long as we don't have to retire around these corpses."

I did my best to suppress a grin but Hermes noticed our smug smiles and frowned at both of us.

"You also know the price for failure. If you fail to return, in all likelihood, life on earth as we know it will perish. But if you return from Arianrhod before obtaining samples of gases, liquids, and solids, and the intelligence for future habitation of it, you will be deprived of your own life in a painful, public manner. Witness this."

At that moment a noise from above caused us to jerk our gaze upward. An enormous rectangular steel platform suspended on a long pole, slowly descended from the ceiling above the table until it hovered like a serving tray inches above the table surface. On top of the platform sat a clear glass dome the size of an inverted bathtub. Inside the dome was a diorama of sorts, a man-made jungle of miniature palms, a pool and grassy hills. And crouching between the fronds of a palm sat a terrified Capuchin monkey.

I glanced at each of the OWL for explanation, but their faces remained impassive. Under the table Rho caught hold of my hand. Though her nails dug into my palm, I squeezed it in reassurance. Then came a shriek of terror from the monkey that tore the breath from my lungs, and with it the feeling of a fist clenching my heart in its grip. Inside the diorama, the pool of water disappeared at the rate of reversed time-lapse photography. The verdant grass and the fronds on the palms browned and withered. In seconds the greenery curled and dried to the point where no moisture remained and it disintegrated into dust. And the monkey...

I had never seen anything like that before and I hope never to again. The monkey screamed in agony. It clawed at its throat and fell to the ground, curled up like a retracted caterpillar. As the monkey desiccated from within, it jerked spasmodically. Then its body split and exploded, covering the interior of the glass box with the paste of its entrails.

To the right of me, Rho made gagging noises as if she were about to reverse swallow. I kicked her under the table. Show any weakness now with what was riding on us, and the privileged classified information we'd been given, and we'd be the human equivalent inside that glass box. Or worse. I snuck a surreptitious glance at the pale faces of my other team mates. We'd all gotten the message. Then the stainless steel tray with its cargo of monkey carnage rose slowly back to the ceiling.

A stone-faced OWL with dark hair, an androgynous figure in the OWL tunic, spoke then. His name plate said Pluto.

"So you see there really is no option other than success. Of course, if you don't make it back to earth," he passed his hand in an all-encompassing gesture to include us, "then in three moons, more or less, all of us left here will meet the same fate as that monkey. And you...well, no one knows what fate you will meet on Arianrhod once your home planet has self-destructed."

And put that way, there weren't a lot of choices

available to us. Especially since earth was now as bare, dusty and dry as that poor monkey's cage.

As we left the room, the last of the OWL, a virtual living statue of female perfection, with a long black braid twisted in a coiled crown around her head, stayed us with an imperious motion of her hand. On anyone else, the movement to her lips could have been construed as a smile, but not from an OWL.

"We believe we have chosen you well. Seek, learn, and come back to us. Make your families proud." Her name was Athena.

Her words struck me as incongruous. Though we'd all been born of traditional families, most of us were orphans, or had no memory of our parents. Nor did we know if we had siblings or cousins, though the OWL kept records to intercept an ill-conceived romance should we inadvertently mate with a close relative. Even those who were fortunate enough to have stayed with their family until the prescribed age of six rotations, were eventually taken from their loved ones and raised in communes by robotic nannies, almost as if they were orphans. Family life was not a destiny for those honored with recruitment by the OWL.

Though we hadn't forgotten the disturbing primate demonstration from the day before, by morning we were buoyed with the anticipation of our mission. We had youth on our side, and a determination to succeed: be heroes and retire to an existence most could only dream about. And we knew too, that if we lagged in any way, Reynard would be behind us, figuratively cracking our backs with whatever method of flogging could be found.

There was another day of preparation to be made before take-off, not the least of which would be fitting each of us for the unique suits that would provide the tenuous cord between life and death should we not discover what we sought on Arianrhod.

An attendant ushered us into an enormous room, more like a warehouse, with row upon row of clothing racks that held the apparel we'd be wearing for the majority of our trip. A female attendant clad in a silver body glove approached and led us to a selection of suits specifically built for the female crew, while the men were taken to another section.

"Looks like Fashion Week," Rho muttered.

On cue, I twirled in front of her like the runway models of rotations gone by.

We stopped at a carousel rack of glimmering full-body suits. Rho and I glanced at each other and laughed out loud in delight. Xi's fingers were already running over the unusual textile of another row of garments, which appeared to be layered with scales.

"The lining is made of Kevlar and the scales are titanium," the attendant explained. "These are the uniforms your commander has commissioned for you to wear when performing your duties outside the ship. They fit over a comfortable body glove similar to mine that you'll wear indoors. Let me demonstrate."

She retrieved a suit that appeared to be her size and unfastened the left side. Kicking off her ankle boots she stepped inside the suit then fastened the clasps and zippers until she was completely enveloped in the shimmering garment.

"I've been told all of you are right-handed, is that correct?" When we nodded she continued, "Come closer and look at the mini-computer on my left sleeve."

On the inside of her left arm was a grid with various squares of multi-colored tabs. "The tabs are marked and should be self-explanatory. For example, the "O" button will increase oxygen intake, but you'll have a tutorial before you begin wearing them to eliminate any questions. The suits are self-regulating, which means that at extreme outside temperatures, such as exposure to high heat, a cooling mechanism keeps your body at the correct body temperature. The same is true in extreme cold: an interior heater will keep you warm. In heat and humidity the scales will self-adjust. Watch this."

She began to jog on the spot, increasing in speed and vigor until her face reddened. As she continued, we saw the scales on the suit raise upward, the way a bird's feathers do when it cools itself. She moved forward to stand in front of a large fan and switched it on. As the breeze from the fan cooled her face the scales lowered until they were once again flush with the suit.

"Wow!" Xi breathed. "That is incredible."

The woman nodded. "Yes, the suit is self-intuitive and will protect you from the elements, even predators, better than anything we've created thus far. We call it the Pangolin, after the spiny anteater."

"So it will protect you from everything?" Rho ventured.

"It's not invincible," the attendant replied. "There are vulnerable spots you need to be aware of." At that she headed toward a row of shelves laden with helmets, boots, and gloves, selecting several.

"Though the scales on the outer part of the suit are made from titanium and extremely durable, your vulnerabilities are where the helmet, gloves, and boots intersect as those can become disconnected from the suit. If you find yourself under attack by a predator the best way to avoid injury is to roll in a fetal position until the attacker moves away. The suit's deodorizing filter prevents your scent from escaping so it's unlikely you'll be tracked."

Each of our faces registered varying degrees of consternation. Though we had confidence in each other, we were flying light years into the unknown with little more than our wits and specialized equipment like the Pangolin to protect us. As the attendant removed the suit we shared amused glances as we let our imaginations run wild about the lack of hygienic opportunities aboard the Astraeus. The attendant shrugged when she saw our grins.

"Your oxygen is replenished much like the method of generating oxygen on board the Astraeus. Through an adaptation of the previous Russian-made Elektron, the oxygen is renewed on demand through electrolysis. A cup in the groin area of your suits allows you to pee into it, which is then directed to a container that splits it into hydrogen and oxygen. The hydrogen is vented outside your suits and the oxygen remains in the holding compartment for breathing."

Rho poked me in the ribs a couple of times so I nudged her not so gently with my foot. Now was not the time to break into childish giggles and look like idiots. I was relieved to see the attendant hadn't noticed.

"As I said, those suits are for when you're outside the ship; there are standard issue uniforms for your comfort indoors. You'll get full briefing and training in the properties of your wearing apparel and equipment tomorrow. We don't anticipate any problems."

While that didn't reassure us much, there wasn't a lot left to ask until after our training. I heard a chortle of laughter coming from another corner of the warehouse and saw the men from our team watching the demonstration of the men's suits. I smiled to myself, thinking about all the practical applications for that suit in everyday life.

If we ever had an everyday life again.

During our flight, which would take a week to cross the 2.7 million light years, each member of the team would be put into a hyperbaric chamber and our bodies held in a catatonic state by means of a curare derivative. This not only made the arduous trip more bearable, it protected us against negative impact upon our organs from crossing time and multiple solar systems at the speed of light. And in fact, we'd been told it would otherwise be difficult to survive the distance and conditions if we did not. Previous missions had disappeared without so much as a satellite blip to indicate what became of them.

In the morning we had a few brief moments together before take-off. Though restless, Rho sat with me for a while. I attempted humor to alleviate her anxiety, which was as palpable as a forcefield. Xi was off with Sig, as they were in the throes of a hot and heavy relationship. The other two men, Omega and Chi were making jokes like 'did you use the restroom?' trying to ease the tension before we would enter our individual chambers for the journey.

"Do you think we're going to make it?" Rho's enormous hazel eyes bore into mine. Like most of earth's people she was of homogeneous race, with olive skin and straight black hair, which she wore cropped to just above her shoulders. Before arriving at Quadrant II as a baby, she'd originated from the northernmost region of Quadrant IV, and had the almond-shaped eyes common to the former residents of China.

I recalled a diagram I'd seen in school where the artist had grouped together row upon row of humans of all ages, sex, and race, lined up in a Fibonacci spiral as if they were colors of the spectrum. And indeed they were: the colors of mankind's spectrum; from the palest skin tones to the swarthiest. In gradients of flesh, most people did not appear much different from the other. And so, even before I was born, the scourge of racism had ended.

Xi's skin tone exuded a natural golden glow as if she'd been out sunbathing, although exposing our skin to the sun in our deteriorated atmosphere was forbidden. Both she and Sig were from the south of Quadrant IV, where the countries of Australia and New Zealand used to be. Though physically fit and muscular as we all were, she had a heavier, fuller figure the males seemed to appreciate. She kept her russet-frosted black hair in a long braid that fell over her shoulder, and her hooded dark eyes gave her a sexy sleepy look.

I was an anomaly. No one knew how far back into my heritage my light blonde hair and eyes, with no more color than water, took me. But I was told I had been born in the northeast portion of Quadrant II, which was formerly made up of European and Scandinavian countries. And as I'd never known my parents, without DNA testing or being granted access to otherwise forbidden birth records, I would never know. Though I stood out because I was 'different', the childhood teasing, speculations about my parentage, and who had impregnated my mother had ultimately been gentle. Discrimination of any kind resulted in the severest of punishments, such as extended sentences to hard manual labor, even for females.

"This is what we've been trained to do," I replied to Rho. "We've rehearsed our roles more than any actor could. We're prepared for equipment malfunctions, unforeseen weather conditions, loss of communication." I shrugged. "And the alternative is that if we don't go, we die anyhow."

I put my arm around Rho and gave her shoulders a

squeeze. "I don't know about you but the carrot they're dangling is quite tempting." The truth was, I had my own apprehensions about the mission, but I wasn't about to taint anyone else's thoughts with my concerns. Caution would be my friend and companion.

Rho's mouth gave a twist as if she were about to reply. Before she could answer an almost symbolic shadow crossed both our faces. Reynard towered above us, his hard unsmiling face containing no hint of emotion, anticipation, or uncertainty. Every time I saw him it made me wonder why the OWL hadn't saved themselves time and money and programmed a robot to do his job.

"Time to go, bitches," he said matter-of-factly. We held back from sharing a glance and rose to our feet as ordered, making our way to the ship, the Astraeus. Named for the Titan god of stars and planets, it was a state of the art scout craft in the shape of a giant moth, with sophisticated living quarters for the crew and a gigantic holding area for the returning specimens we'd be gathering. Well designed for its purpose.

Captain Reynard handed us each a small paper cup of syrupy fluid and a tablet to swallow that would put us into our catatonic state for a week. I glanced at the bright overhead clock that read: T-90. We had ninety days to get to Planet A, collect the samples, and return before all the inhabitants on earth would suffer the same fate as the Capuchin monkey. It seemed like both an eternity and a death sentence.

After giving each other a hug and final salute for good luck, we folded ourselves into our chamber, a sarcophagus-like apparatus that would supply us with oxygen and nutrients to keep up our strength. They would also serve as our beds while on Arianrhod. When we landed the clock should read T-83, which would mean that we'd spent a week traveling through the galaxy. As Captain Reynard closed our doors, our eyes shut automatically in response to the drug. Then presumably, he too, took a tablet and entered his chamber where he would stay until the craft landed on Planet A.

II

I awoke to the most crippling nausea I'd ever experienced and a pounding in my head more violent than any migraine. The worst of it was that I was in a forced horizontal position with no way to double up to counteract the vertigo and cramps. Whether something had gone wrong with my absorption of the tablet or we were already on Planet A, I couldn't tell. Nor could I tell if anyone else was experiencing the same phenomena. The hatches to the hyperbaric chambers were programmed to be released automatically upon landing. So how long I would be stuck in this position, I had no way of knowing.

Time passed by at a crawl. In my discomfort, all I could do was lie there and wait until the programming took over, which seemed interminable as time had no measurement. What appeared to me to be hours might have only been minutes. There was no way to tell. But then, in what could have been days or only hours, almost as if I had willed it, my chamber door slowly opened on its own volition and I was free to step outside. Even so, I waited for several moments, as I'd been trained, to determine if the air was still breathable within the ship.

When it became apparent that it was safe to move outside my chamber I disengaged my life support connectors and crawled out. The nausea still held me tight in its grip, but now an enormous dizziness and sense of falling overwhelmed me even more. Gripping the sides of the chamber I pulled myself free and sat on the edge of the stainless steel framework, collecting my bearings as I surveyed the rest of the stateroom.

It appeared that I was the only one who had emerged so far, yet our chambers had been programmed to simultaneously open upon landing, coinciding with the wearing off of the tablet we'd taken. I glanced around the dimly lit room, the muted light shedding an orangey tinge from the chambers that helped keep our bodies at an even temperature. All the other chamber doors except mine remained closed. I moved into the bridge and headed toward one of the ship's computer terminals, pressing the power button as I watched it boot to life. It was then that I noticed that the clock above the monitors read T-85. If the calculations of earth's Command Unit Base, or CUB as we called it, had been correct, my chamber should not have opened for another two days.

How I would pass my time for another forty-eight hours without active instructions from Reynard or CUB worried me. Still, what could I do? I was awake and out of my chamber, and the rest of my team were not. At least, I assumed they weren't, but in truth, I had yet to look.

The thought of seeing my teammates lying there like corpses in their coffins made me shudder but I forced myself to return to the sleeping area in the stateroom to see. I easily found Rho and Xi because I'd watched them enter their chambers. Then I went to the opposite section and found Sig, Omega, and Chi. Though decidedly chilling, there was comfort knowing my teammates were still there, intact, waiting for the cue from the ship. There was another chamber besides mine, of course, and though the lid was closed I found the chamber empty. That was where the lanky form of Captain Reynard should have been. But wasn't.

For a moment my heartbeat seemed to ricochet in alarm. I headed toward the bridge and moved over to the Astraeus' main operating computer and sat at the keyboard, willing myself to be calm. Without Captain Reynard we had no immediate leader or direction. And why he would not be in a chamber like the rest of us defied logic. We were given to understand that he would have followed the procedure that the rest of us had.

After I'd had a while to think about it, I decided that the best way to resolve my questions was to find Reynard. We'd familiarized ourselves with the layout of the Astraeus during our training, as well as doing walk-throughs well before takeoff, so locating him shouldn't be a problem. If, in fact, he had actually boarded the ship after we had.

The Astraeus' floor plan consisted of the bridge from where we controlled communications, as well as take-off and landing, the staterooms that contained our sleeping/transport chambers, the computer room, the engineering area that controlled the engine and landing gear, and the airlock, from which we would exit the ship. There was also an equipment room between the stateroom and engineering that contained the supplies that would sustain us for the next three moons. Behind the stateroom were two large cargo bays that would hold all the samples we were to collect from Planet A. I went to each room in turn. Though lighting should have been unnecessary to us during our voyage, therefore leaving the ship dark or strictly dimmed to conserve power, the running lights at floor level, and the room at the rear were brightly lit. It was there, the engineering room, I ventured into after crossing through the staterooms to leave the bridge. And it was there I found Captain Reynard.

He glanced up as I entered. A deep frown furrowed his brows, quickly disappearing when he saw it was me. A military man all the way, his graying 'high and tight' Marine-style haircut that contrasted sharply with his leather-brown complexion, seemed as if readied for a Campaign cover, his demeanor as stiff as his Control-issued uniform. If Reynard had initially been surprised to see me, he did not appear unduly alarmed. Despite the fact he was my superior in this mission, until thoroughly explained, his being here out of his chamber made me suspicious.

"Ah, I see you've awakened early," he said as if it were normal procedure, when in fact I knew it was not. Our team had been informed that it was highly unlikely, as well as dangerous, for anyone to awaken and emerge from their chambers before landing on Planet A. Apparently we'd been misled on that piece of information.

"And so have you," I countered.

He nodded. "The team wasn't told that I would be awake a full three days before everyone else. This was so I could take atmospheric readings and make certain we were on the correct trajectory. If I'd been in a catatonic state like the rest of you, and we'd landed in a different place or in such a way that was not part of the program, it would be detrimental to the mission. Instead, I was to monitor directional systems early to make certain everything went according to plan."

While his words rang true, there was something about the delivery that seemed contrived and insincere. Yet I couldn't put my finger on it. I had no reason not to believe him. Still, I felt the Control Unit Base might have briefed us about this. But perhaps that was also part of the plan. In my recent reactivation into normalcy, who was I to question him? So I shrugged and said, "What do we need to do for the next 48-hours before we land?"

He smiled, and if I hadn't mentioned before that he had a smile that was neither friendly nor reassuring, I'm mentioning it now. "Just follow my lead," he said. And to that command I had no rebuttal.

During the next two days spent with Captain Reynard, I assisted in calculating our landing and take-off coordinates, worked out how we'd obtain samples and readings from the planet, survive the ordeal, and return to earth, not necessarily in that order. Without additional companionship, I found myself beginning to enjoy his company. His was a dry, almost nonexistent, military sense of humor. He liked things done his way and if not challenged or questioned, then life went along smoothly. If you objected to his methods or when asked to perform a task, then you'd better be prepared for the ice-cold glare of his deeply set black eyes. Eyes that could hold you riveted the way a snake stares down a rat. You knew you were doomed before you started so you just didn't go there. It was that simple.

Attempts to engage him in conversation about his background, training, or personal life were met with a deft changing of the subject. He was so adept at it that I found myself sharing pieces about my own life, and my plans for the future once we were back on our home planet. He did volunteer information that afterwards I felt was inadvertent: his concern about the lack of intel we had on Planet A. We knew about the high ratio of hydrogen gas. We'd been briefed about the likely absence of life forms similar to ours but with luck the ability to sustain life due to the region's ESI. But it was what we didn't know that concerned him. And if he was concerned, we needed to be even more so.

By the time the rest of the crew was to awaken and we were within hours of landing, Captain Reynard ordered me into my chamber to ease the discomfort of entering the planet's atmosphere.

"Are you doing the same?" I asked then added, "were you ever in the chamber or had you been lucid for the entire journey until I woke up?"

He gave me a hard look. "What difference does it make? I'm your captain on this mission. I know my role. You take my orders and you don't ask questions. So now, Recruit, enter your chamber or you will be wishing you'd listened to me when you had the chance."

I obeyed him because that was what I'd been trained to do, though now I wish I hadn't. But as they say, hindsight is 20/20. So I followed him to the stateroom and folded myself back into my chamber. Then he fastened the chamber lid. And what happened between that moment and the landing, of which I was blissfully unaware, I could not say. I didn't even have the benefit of a tablet to stabilize my mind and body.

T-83

I felt, rather than heard, the lid of my chamber open. I lay there for a moment waiting for any indication the rest of the team was awake. When I heard the other chamber doors opening, followed by the thudding of feet hitting the floor as they emerged, I raised myself up like a vampire from a coffin and glanced around.

Rho and Xi were on their feet. Rho rubbed her eyes

as if coming out of a deep sleep; Xi looked blurry-eyed and disoriented. The men appeared unperturbed and bounced from their chambers. Sig, whose baby face and wiry build made him appear much younger than the rest of us, staggered a bit as he hit the floor, causing a ripple of laughter from the others.

"How did you manage to get drunk when the rest of us were sleeping?" Omega teased.

It surprised me that Captain Reynard was nowhere to be seen though I said nothing to the rest of the team about the forty-eight hours we'd spent together while they were obliviously sleeping. When we had gathered our bearings, we headed to the bridge. Reynard was waiting for us, drumming his fingers impatiently on the ship's console until we were all assembled and standing at attention.

"I know you think you feel fine," he said, "but Sig will check everyone's vital signs before we suit up and venture outside. If any of you are not completely stable you'll have to remain inside the ship until I think it's safe for you to join the rest of us."

Though we all had strict instructions to obey, a round of groans followed his announcement. Even so, no one had the guts to challenge his orders. Instead we lined up like preschoolers in kindergarten as we'd been trained to do, in order of rank, with me standing next to Omega. As our medical officer, Sig proceeded to take our temperatures, check our pulse and heart rate, and felt our lymph nodes for swelling. When he pronounced every one of us fit for duty, and once Reynard had checked Chi's vitals, we were free to suit up.

Seven crew members, two small staterooms; there was no margin for shyness or modesty. This was how we'd all grown up. Sexuality only played a part when in privacy between two people (assuming that was the way you rolled). We stripped, cleaned up and helped each other climb into our Pangolin suits, complete with breathing apparatus. Omega had suited up first, and as his body temperature warmed inside the suit, the scales began to rise up for ventilation.

"Are those your scales or are you just happy to see me?" I joked, causing his face to flush and the scales on his suit to rise even higher. While the others laughed, Omega turned away and busied himself with packing our supplies to hide his embarrassment.

Once we'd suited up, we made our way back to the bridge. Rho took current readings of the atmospheric conditions outside the Astraeus. The rest of us arranged ourselves in a semicircle and stood in silence while we waited for her findings before heading out. As she punched in calculation after calculation, Reynard finally became impatient.

"How does it look?" he asked, "Is there anything we need to be worried about?"

Rho swiveled in her chair and faced him. "I have to recalibrate the equipment and recalculate the entire readout." Briefly she turned back to the monitor screen. "For some reason the readings aren't even close to what the Control Unit Base predicted. I don't understand how they could be so far off."

"Let me take a look," Reynard growled, pushing on her shoulder, a little too roughly it seemed to me, to move her from the chair. She shot him a look but stood so he could scrutinize the monitor.

"If you look at the printout you'll see what I'm talking about," Rho huffed. "The atmospheric pressure is as predicted, but the oxygen levels were supposed to be much higher. Close to breathable. But they're scarcely discernible. We knew the hydrogen level was going to be abnormally high, it's at 90%, but there are other inert gases as well."

"What does that mean for us when we're out there working?" Chi asked. Of all of us, Chi was a bit of an enigma. Though he could always be counted on to follow orders, or pitch in to help or complete what he started, he never interacted much socially. It seemed an anomaly for a young man so startlingly handsome, with his flawless bone structure and darker toned skin. His reticence seemed to confound Rho, who had kept her crush on him secret from everyone else except me.

Reynard moved away from the computer monitor. "It means that the air here is not breathable, at least not the location we are at right now. Study the readings on Rho's printout. It's imperative that the oxygen feed levels in your helmets are adjusted to compensate for the hostile atmosphere outside the ship."

With those comments he grabbed a sheaf of papers from the printer, handing a readings sheet to each of the team. Then he and the others headed back to the equipment room to continue packing the gear we'd need to start collecting our samples. I hung back for several moments, watching them as they engaged in cheerful banter until they disappeared from view. Rho had resumed her post at the computer, plugging away at numbers again. I bent over her shoulder to take a look. There was something in her demeanor that gave me a feeling of unease.

I put my hand on her shoulder to get her attention. "What is it that you're not telling us?"

She shook her head slowly. "I wish I knew. It's not possible for our atmospheric readings to be so far off what we were told they'd be when we arrived. It's almost as if we didn't land on the right planet."

"What!" It came out louder than I intended, causing her to raise her finger to her lips to quiet me. "What?" I repeated.

She turned around completely and stared up at me. "Don't say anything to the rest of the team. I need to send out a communication with our readings to CUB anyhow, so I'll let you know what I find out." She hesitated for a moment.

"It could be as simple as a missing piece of data. Or maybe we had landed on another area of the planet from what we'd projected, which could give us false readings." Her eyes pleaded with mine and I could see concern lying behind their hazel depths. "Be cautious out there, Zeta. And watch your back."

It occurred to me then to ask what she was trying to warn me about when I heard the word 'bitches!' shouted out and realized Reynard was barking orders, possibly wondering where I was. Before he could call out my name I headed to the equipment room and found the rest of the team ready to disembark. I grabbed my gear and fell in line behind the rest, leaving Rho to finish her transmission to CUB before she came to join us.

As we made our way along the corridor, the ceiling lights shining down on the glistening titanium suits formed dancing rainbows along the walls of the ship. The insulation in the suit fascinated me; it protected our bodies both from extreme heat or cold, keeping us at a comfortable 37 degrees Celsius inside the suit. But of course, the true test of the suit and helmet with its atmospheric controls would be when we stepped outside.

With Captain Reynard leading, we trudged toward the airlock and through the massive cargo bays where we'd be storing samples of whatever we found. Omega was the last to leave, being the highest in rank after Captain Reynard. In our identical suits and with our similar body structure it was difficult to differentiate the others save for the identifying symbols upon our helmets. Smiling or making facial expressions was virtually pointless for no one could really see you. However, the mouthpiece had a speaker on the helmet with an exterior dial that could be turned up to project your voice, should you need more volume. From what I could hear, Reynard had his cranked up nearly all the way.

We grouped outside the ship in our customary semicircle and waited for the cue to begin loading the Explorer, the larger of our two ATVs, and cart with testing equipment needed to collect our samples and prepare them for storage. Because of their potential contamination and possible volatility, the materials would remain in outside holding tanks until they were verified to be stable. No one wanted to be burned up in their sleep or shattered like a dropped frozen ice bar should one element react with another. As chemist, it would be my job to ascertain that whatever we brought back to the ship would be safe to transport home to earth.

After Reynard's go-ahead, we loaded the equipment required for obtaining and temporarily storing the specimens onto a cart that would be pulled by the Explorer. From our training we knew how to proceed without further direction and split into two groups. Along with Rho and Omega, I would be part of the exploratory team, the chemist doing preliminary testing of anything we'd be bringing back. More in-depth testing would take place once we got the stuff back to earth. The other team, consisting of Xi, Sig and Chi, would go back and prepare what we managed to collect. Not unlike ancient hunters who brought back the kill so the women and children could prepare it and store it for the winter. Captain Reynard would oversee all and become a part of each team when or if we needed assistance.

III

Omega backed the Explorer expertly down the ramp of the Astraeus, whereupon Sig hitched to it the rolling cart already loaded with our equipment and storage containers. When Reynard wasn't looking, I took a moment to slack off and take in what would be our home for the next two moons, if we were lucky enough not to become marooned here. Planet A was probably the most beautiful place I'd ever seen. In the ambient light from the Astraeus and the Explorer, the abundance of hydrogen gas gave it a luminous blue glow along the horizon, while nearer us a gentle iridescent violet warmed the cool blueness of our suits. It was like being in the center of neon lights, reminding me of old photos I'd seen of a place that had long ago disappeared into oblivion called the Las Vegas strip.

The planet itself lacked any real light other than the luminescent glow, so no shadows darkened the view. Low jagged peaks of rock formations that were probably grey, though shone a purplish hue from the hydrogen, roughened the landscape. It was not unlike the coral reefs that had existed in earth's oceans before pollution took its toll and killed off all the sea life. And then the oceans had run dry. The landscape of Arianrhod had all the surrealism of a Salvador Dali painting.

I watched as the team finished organizing the gear in the trailer and at that moment caught Reynard glaring at me. I jumped in to help before he could yell at me. Soon we were all ready to leave, Omega driving, while Rho and I sat beside and behind him respectively. Our goal was to collect as many rock and mineral samples as we could in the containers and bring them back to the ship. From there we'd make trip after trip over the following weeks until we had filled the ship's cargo bays to capacity.

The Command Unit Base on earth had estimated it would take us nearly two moons to complete the mission if we worked around the clock. And as this planet had neither night nor day, working in shifts was how they'd structured the goal. Upon our return we would have enough specimens to determine if Arianrhod would be habitable enough to colonize. Once the planet's safety was established, another team would be sent out and begin building settlements. Inevitably, additional teams would follow, until we'd completely annihilated one more source for our needs. Then we'd be exploring the solar system for yet another planet to pillage. It didn't seem right to me, but then I wasn't one of the OWL. And I wanted to survive as much as the next person.

Omega maneuvered the craft along the rocky sur-face, the air-equipped ride gliding along as if we were in a hovercraft, though the wheels never left the rocky planet surface. A smooth ride was essential for bringing in our samples as there were likely substances previously undis-covered that could detonate our cargo given the right cir-cumstances. None of us wanted to become a part of the atmosphere should the entire craft hit a large rock and explode.

We had already traveled several miles from the ship and though I hadn't said anything to my team, I was reluctant to get too far away. We hadn't definitively established that there weren't any existing life forms on this planet, hostile or otherwise. If there were inhabitants, we needed to know they would not be life threatening. Of course, we had been told there were none. But having watched many space exploration documentaries as a child, I remained unconvinced. Fictional alien life had the ability to infiltrate everything.

The readout equipment I carried on my lap squeaked, and the LED numbers lit up the screen, indicating that large concentrations of hydrogen, as well as other residual peripheral gases, were nearby. There was still no reading for oxygen. Omega slowed the craft and half-turned to me in question. I nodded. He pulled to a stop and we all piled out and started setting up our equipment.

Then just for a moment I thought I saw a flicker of light glint off one of the rocks. But this was impossible as there were no light sources. Any illumination, other than the existing glow, would come from the beams from our helmets and suits, in addition to the headlamps from our craft. Possibly even a reflection off any of them. After I failed to see anything else, I shrugged off the notion. We busied ourselves with the task of lifting soil and rock samples, testing and calculating, then harvesting; testing and calculating, and harvesting.

We'd worked for several hours when I felt Omega touch my arm.

"Let's take a break," came through his mouth speaker. "No sense in killing ourselves off the first day."

I nodded and reached over to tap Rho, who appeared to have already heard him. We moved toward the Explorer and sat on the sides of the trailer. Omega hauled out several flasks with protruding straws that would fit through the mouthpieces of our helmets. Through that we replenished our fluid and caloric needs via a high protein substance that tasted like cherry soda, or like KoolAid from long ago. There was an historic irony in that thought, which I quickly managed to forget because once again I thought I saw a small light behind a distant rock formation.

"Did you see that?" I asked Rho, but the question was pointless as she'd had her back to the direction from which it came.

"What are you talking about?" Omega asked, glancing around.

"That's the second time I thought I saw a light and a movement. Nothing much. But enough that it caught my attention."

He thought about that for a few moments. "There may be phosphorescence in the rocks. The glow from the hydrogen might make it appear to be shining, depending on which angle you're looking from." I could see his dark almond-shaped eyes examining me closely through his visor. "It's probably more your imagination than anything. Being out here in a place completely foreign and unknown to us all would spook anyone."

I bristled with indignation. Although Omega outranked me, I rarely acknowledged the fact, often going about the job I knew so well without seeking direction. I realized that annoyed him to a degree. He'd also made a few passes at me that I'd rejected before we were recruited for this mission. But then neither he nor anyone else knew about Lucian. I hadn't been too thrilled he'd been part of my team, but decided to be professional about the whole thing. Was making me feel vulnerable his way of getting back at me? I fought down the notion.

"I wasn't spooked," I objected. "I only wondered if anyone else had seen it and if they knew what it might be." I gave him a sugary sweet smile he couldn't see behind my mouthpiece. "You're probably right, though, it was most likely my imagination." When he wasn't looking in my direction I gave Rho a nudge with my gloved hand and she gave me a wink. We'd be all right, us two.

When we'd finally filled up the containers in the cart, Omega turned the Explorer around and we made our way back to the Astraeus. There we found Xi, Sig and Chi awaiting our arrival in the engineering room. Rho and I jumped from the Explorer while Omega drove it back to where they'd be preparing our raw materials for pre-shipping. Seeing only the three of them, I glanced around.

"Where's Reynard?"

At that moment Omega emerged from the airlock. We all stared at each other until Omega, who hadn't noticed Reynard wasn't present when he entered the room, turned sharply.

"Reynard's not here?" Omega asked, concern weighing his voice down to a growl.

Xi shrugged. "He left a couple of hours ago, said he wanted to scout the periphery on his own. He's got emergency flares and survival equipment with him."

I turned to Sig. "And his leaving on his own didn't seem strange to any of you? Our orders were to travel in groups of no less than two, and never, under any circumstances, to venture out solo."

"Not really," he responded, "he said he'd return before anyone missed him."

My thoughts flew back to when I'd awoken earlier

than the prepared-for duration and found Reynard awake and wandering around the ship. Not for the first time I questioned his motives. Though in the two days we'd spent together planning the mission without any of the others involved, we'd gotten to know each other's habits and personalities, if not our backgrounds. And that part concerned me. As a commanding officer and leader of the team, he knew everything there was to know about us, while we knew virtually nothing of him.

I thought about telling the others what I hadn't shared with anyone: that I had been awake for two days earlier on board the ship than they had. And Reynard, despite what he said, had more than likely been awake and doing God knows what the entire journey. Before I could tell them about it though, I heard his voice booming through the encampment.

"What the hell are you bitches standing around for?"

We jumped back as if we were little children caught sneaking candy. But we weren't. We were a team of choreographed professionals, and despite my earlier feelings that we had gotten along fairly well when we were alone on board ship together, I started resenting him. He seemed to add nothing to the team. We did all the grunt work while he went off doing what only he knew. And I got the sense the rest of the team felt the same way. But we said nothing; we followed orders and proceeded with our tasks again like the automatons we were.

That evening, despite the lack of privacy, Rho and I had a moment alone to talk while Chi and Reynard walked the periphery for any sign of potential problems, or alien life forms.

"I need to talk to you," I whispered so Xi wouldn't hear us. I wasn't worried about her anyhow because, out of sight of Reynard, she was deep in a lip lock on top of

Sig, who lay on his back in his chamber. Although personal relationships weren't frowned upon, overt demonstrations of affection while on active missions were against protocol and regulations. Somewhat embarrassed, I felt like dropping the lid on them and smothering them both. But for now it was useful to have them otherwise occupied so Rho and I could talk. Omega was in his chamber catching up on sleep until it was time for his patrol.

Rho looked troubled. "What is it?" I glanced around to make sure no one was listening in, or sneaky Reynard wasn't lurking in the corners of the crew's quarters.

"I wasn't in stasis for the entire seven days of the flight." Her eyes widened in alarm, but she said nothing. "And neither was Reynard. In fact, he was up and around when I awoke at T-85."

She frowned. Her beautiful hazel eyes searched mine. "Why would we all stay catatonic and not you and Reynard?"

I shook my head. "As for me, I can't tell you. Maybe there's something resistant in my body chemistry, just like the way I'm, uh,"—I didn't know quite how to say it, so I went ahead and said it—"a little different from the rest of you."

She snorted. "So you're blonde. Big deal. I've met other blondes before. Not many because it's a throwback gene. You're not that special and you're not that different."

I gave a short laugh. "Thanks a lot. What an ego-booster. What I meant was that maybe something in my personal makeup, because I'm light skinned or whatever my gene pool dictates, made me react differently. Perhaps I was more resistant to the drug than the rest of you. I woke up two days early. That wasn't supposed to happen."

Her mouth twisted. "Why would that happen with Reynard?" She studied my face. "Did something occur between you two while you were awake?"

"No, NO! Of course not," I blurted.

Maybe I spoke too hastily, because in truth nothing had happened. Nor would it ever.

"But," I paused, gnawing on my lip, "he said he'd awakened the day before I did. I actually think he'd been awake, or at least not catatonic, the entire voyage."

"That wasn't the plan." Rho's voice was terse. "That's not the procedure the Control Team prepared us for during our training."

"No, it's not. And that's why I can't help but wonder what he's up to. I think…"

"What do you think?" Reynard's caustic voice cut through my words like a sword. "Tell us, Zeta, what it is you're thinking?"

I swiveled and met his eyes dead on, without wavering.

"I think that there are others on this planet besides us," I said.

It was the only response I could come up with instantaneously to cover up the conversation. I could feel everyone's eyes on me, even Omega who had sat straight up in his chamber when he heard Reynard, and Xi and Sig, who in the space of a heartbeat had managed to put half the room between them.

Reynard stared at me then, his coal black eyes narrowing as he gave me that soulless smile. "Now that's just preposterous, Zeta," he said. "Keep talking that way and you'll be confined to the ship, filling in the log book instead of out there in the field, doing the important work."

My face burned with shame and anger at being chas-

tised in front of my teammates. I wondered if he'd overheard me. And if so, was his comment a false flag, a way
of deflecting attention from my suspicions? I kept my
gaze lowered as they all sidled away in collective embarrassment for me, and only glanced up when Omega
squeezed my shoulder as he passed.

IV

With the rest of the team avoiding any sort of contact with me, the next day seemed excruciatingly long, especially given my particular tasks: locating anything that gave out new readings on my equipment, preliminarily testing it for volatility, and doing the same thing over and over again. I contemplated the luxury of staying in the ship and writing logs and compiling statistics, though I knew that Reynard would probably never let that happen. It wasn't what I had been trained for and I was far too valuable to have my talents wasted on paperwork only to make an example of me.

However, my job was nothing if not labor intensive. Over the course of the day I found myself overwhelmingly exhausted. We'd go at it for four hours, rest for a six-hour stretch, alternate by taking turns at patrol, then be back at collecting specimens again for another four hours. I dreaded the idea of the next seven or more weeks. It might have been tolerable had Captain Reynard been less of a taskmaster. But it became apparent that his skills lay in those of a drill sergeant, not as a team player whose job was to motivate a group of young scientists while they collected substances that would determine whether earth's remaining inhabitants would live on.

I watched for signs of dissension among my team members. But then, I wondered, even if everyone else was as disenchanted as me with Reynard, what would we do? Mutiny? And for what purpose? It wasn't as if we could take him prisoner until the mission had ended. Because then we'd be court-martialed when we returned to earth, and end up as monkey butter inside a bell jar. But he never let up and things got steadily worse.

In such close quarters as the way we lived on board the Astraeus, it would be difficult not to notice things going on around you. I soon became aware that Xi and Sig no longer appeared to be a couple. In fact, when one was in the room, the other moved away as if polarized. Though I wondered at the cause I was secretly relieved. I'd had to make the same sacrifice by putting my budding relationship with Lucian on hold until my return. Romance can color and complicate emotions—we didn't need more drama that we already had, light years away from our home planet.

T-75

I rolled over in my chamber, trying to get comfortable and take advantage of my last hour of break when I heard a thumping on the open chamber lid that caused me to sit bolt upright.

"Time for a meeting." Reynard announced. "I'm restructuring the teams, bitches. We're meeting in the bridge."

Still groggy, I stumbled from my chamber, my feet holding me up unsteadily as I struggled into my bodysuit.

I stole a glance at the others who had been asleep. Several of them mumbled under their breath. I grabbed a handful of caffeinated energy serum packets as we passed through the common area and distributed them to the rest of the team. When we'd all assembled in the bridge, rubbing our eyes and yawning, sucking on our energy packets, Reynard allowed his gaze to rest on each of us for several moments.

"I've been examining the log books and our productivity is decreasing, not increasing the way it should be. I think our current teams are spending too much time visiting and less working. Becoming too reliant on any one team member makes you weak and vulnerable, especially if we were to meet hostile elements. So I've taken into consideration your individual strengths and weaknesses and here's the line-up until further notice."

He turned to me: "Zeta, you and Sig will be collecting specimens in Sector 3 while Xi and Chi do the chemical analysis. Rho will stay with the ship, monitoring communications and logging in the reports." While we all stared at each other, dumbfounded, he turned to Omega.

"You will accompany me on exploratory missions. We will be looking further afield from our current operations for changes in terrain while the others are harvesting the local samples."

Once again his cold-eyed glance lingered on each of us in turn, long enough to bore the unspoken threat into our minds. "I need all of you to be on your toes should anything unplanned take place."

I couldn't help wondering if he himself had something 'planned,' but refrained from remarking upon it as it would only result in harder labor. At what point, I mused, had we gone from being a team led by Reynard, to becoming his personal slaves?

We were about to disassemble once he gave the cue, but instead froze in place by his frown and sudden 'at attention' stance we'd come to beware of. As I took in his arrogance I realized how much I'd come to loathe the man. I wondered if the others felt the same. But as I shared glances with each of them I saw their faces were without expression as they listened intently to his words.

"You're not dismissed yet, bitches. Because production has slowed so much, I'm also increasing the length of your shifts. Instead of collecting samples for four hours and sleeping for six, until further notice we'll reverse the procedure. You'll be exploring for six hours and allowed four hours sleep. We'll be working around the clock."

For a few moments he stared at the ceiling, tapping on his chin, deliberately keeping us in suspense and increasing annoyance. Finally he said, "One more thing. I want all of you to cross-train each other with your jobs. That way should anything happen to one of our team the other will be able to step in without so much as a bleep on the radar."

An indescribably sick sensation started to form in the bottom of my stomach, though I couldn't exactly say why. I noticed that the rest of the team appeared particularly uncomfortable. Couldn't he see that decreasing our sleep and making us work longer hours would only lower productivity, not raise it? Reynard flashed us his lovely smile once more before dismissing us.

"I don't think I need to remind you that failure is not an option. We cannot go back without providing evidence of a new and hospitable homeland."

His hardened gaze traveled the room and settled on me last. Almost as if he were speaking to me in private, he said, "If we can't return with proof, we WILL not return." Then I understood his madness.

I didn't dare glance at any of the crew. These changes were a devastating and demoralizing move on Reynard's part. With harvesting more and sleeping less we'd be exhausted to the point of failure. Cross training would take time, which would in turn slow down production. What was he thinking? Something would have to give; something would have to break. I just didn't know what.

My new team now consisted of Xi, Chi and Sig. Rho, ordered to stay with the craft and perform the tedious logging and reports of our samples, managed to force back the tears that threatened to surface when we left her alone in the ship. Why Omega had become Reynard's shadow, and would be following him like a puppy on whatever 'exploratory treks' Reynard made, I couldn't say. And despite my occasional discomfort around Omega, as our second-in-command I missed his experience and authority, though we all knew our jobs well enough to perform without supervision.

Although Xi and I had never been close, her avoiding Sig afforded me more opportunity to train her to do my job, answering her questions and working as speedily as possible so as to not come up short in production. She, in turn, trained me in hers, which was to label and categorize everything we located. Eventually we all reclaimed our original rhythm and the operation returned to a relative normalcy.

One day when we were alone together in the stateroom and I felt enough at ease with Xi to talk about personal matters I asked, "What happened between you and Sig? You two seemed destined for a permanent coupling."

She gave a slight shrug and glanced away. It was the most emotion I'd seen out of her; she wasn't a softhearted person like Rho, and from what I had seen she'd never gone out of her way to do a kindness for anyone. Still, I felt a rush of sympathy because she seemed to be hurting.

"Reynard told us it could potentially harm the mission; make us vulnerable if we had personal feelings towards team members. He said that's why he keeps rotating us, so we don't form close bonds or relationships."

I thought about that for a moment. He was right, in a way, though I believed that forming bonds would in turn make the team stronger. Only my opinion, of course, and not one I'd dare voice to him.

"How did Sig feel about it?"

"He said maybe Captain Reynard was right. Besides, it was only for another few weeks because once we'd completed the mission we'd be free to be together. So we agreed that until we got back to earth we'd give the appearance that we were a done deal and Reynard wouldn't have anything more to say."

She smiled shyly and raised her left hand in front of my face, wiggling her fingers like a child. "He gave me this as something to hold onto until we could officially be together."

Her extended hand sported an OWL Academy ring, an opal held in place by the four clasps depicting the Quadrants. I'd seen Sig wearing it. He would have received it after graduating from medical training. Customarily, anyone placing a ring of that importance on an intended's finger meant it as a gesture of permanence.

"I gave him my Academy ring in return," she said, almost to herself. "Only mine has a star sapphire in the center. We are bound together in this mission and afterward, no matter where it takes us."

I nodded, trying to understand. Until Lucian, I'd never even had a crush so a commitment such as theirs was a relatively foreign concept to me, an unnecessary tethering of emotions in an uncertain world.

Still, their trial separation sounded like the best thing all around given our close quarters and backbreaking work load. Maybe it would be a good test for their relationship, too. If they survived this temporary separation their affection could grow into love, if it wasn't at that stage already. It surprised me that Reynard had put Xi and Sig on the same team, although knowing how he operated, it was probably a test.

But now I realized why Rho was on desk duty and not with me out in the field. Reynard knew we were friends; he probably thought we were lovers, though we weren't. Divide and conquer seemed to be his latest and most effective method of operation.

"Just make sure that Reynard doesn't notice you're wearing each other's rings," I cautioned.

A couple of days later while working with Sig, I remarked, "Xi told me that Reynard put the brakes on your relationship. I'm sorry."

He didn't reply, instead nodded toward the specimen tray I had already laid out when we arrived at Sector Two. I reached for a fresh container from the half-filled row and opened it. He dropped a sample of rock into the container with his tweezers and cleaned the tip before inserting it back into his kit. Straightening his back, he tilted his head and smiled at me.

"We'll get over it. It's not forever. We exchanged rings."

I nodded, turning to catalog the sample he'd just taken. When I finished, I sealed the container and turned back to him.

"Do you think switching up the teams is really due to productivity, or something larger?"

Sig studied me for a few minutes. Once again I marveled at his baby-faced good looks. He and Xi were an attractive, though contrasting couple. I found myself wondering if their relationship would survive Reynard's directives. Their forced rift made for awkwardness in our group.

"I don't know," he responded slowly. "I keep questioning why Reynard was chosen for this mission. There were plenty of other commanders in our training program and in the OWL regime. Some of the others I worked with believed they would be chosen. It came as a surprise when they were passed over for Reynard."

"Did I hear my name mentioned?" My breath felt as if it were sucked out of my lungs. Sig and I exchanged quick glances before we turned in unison to see Reynard standing near the Explorer, hands on his hips. How he'd arrived without making a sound, I had no idea. Perhaps he'd been close by the whole while, watching us working, seeing if Xi and Sig interacted romantically.

Sig, nonconfrontational as always, took the easy way out, busying himself with organizing and packing up his equipment to put in the Explorer.

I smiled at Reynard, though my heart still beat irregularly in my chest at his sudden appearance.

"We were just saying how much more sense the current teams make," I said, giving him a guileless smile. "I think we've catalogued more samples today than since we arrived."

Reynard's face was a mask of inscrutable slyness. He gave us a curt nod and climbed into the back of the Explorer as he waited for us to finish loading our gear.

V

T-70

A few days later the line-up morphed again as Reynard decided to take Sig with him on his 'walkabout.' I could see that Sig was extremely uncomfortable with this. There had to be other reasons besides what he'd told me that had him avoiding being alone with Reynard and staying as far in the background as possible. It wasn't only because Reynard had put the kibosh on his relationship with Xi. But knowing Reynard as I was beginning to, any number of valid reasons could account for Sig's apparent distaste for the man.

"What is it you do out there when you go on your 'exploratory missions?'" I asked Omega, once Reynard and Sig were out of sight and earshot.

"Wouldn't you like to know?" I could hear the childish smirk in his voice. He still hadn't gotten over my rebuffing his advances.

"Well, yes, I would like to know, that's why I asked."

While we were talking I kept working. I had no intention of letting anyone who might be more loyal to Reynard than to me as a team member report that I was slacking off. The truth was that I didn't know where Omega's allegiances lay. I knew he was ambitious. But I also thought he still harbored a romantic interest toward me, evidenced by catching his eyes lingering on me longer than necessary when he thought I didn't notice. So I used this to my advantage. I laughed and gave him a wink, which was the only part of my face through my helmet where he could see my expression.

As I had cross-trained him in my job also, he moved up and began working alongside my area.

"Keep this between us," he whispered conspiratorially. "He tried to hit on me."

I burst out laughing, almost dropping my tools. "Shut up!"

He sniggered. "Yeah, I'm making that up. Seriously, though, he told me not to share this with the rest of you. He's looking for phosphorite."

I stopped and straightened up from my work, staring at him in wonderment. After the wars, the greatest problem facing the planet was how to fertilize crops to feed the population. Earth's phosphorus sources had depleted to alarming levels even before the formation of the OWL. The world's largest phosphorus mines had long been stripped. The shortage reached the point to where toilets had been modified to collect urine to process the residual phosphorus from it. It would be nothing short of miraculous to discover a new source of phosphorus to take back to a planet on the verge of extinction because of limited natural resources.

"Phosphorite? Why? That's not what the OWL and the Control Team sent us here to collect. We're harvesting all sorts of specimens to substantiate colonizing a new planet. If it exists here we'll discover it in the soil samples we're collecting. From what we've seen so far, though, there is nothing growing, ergo, there is no phosphorus present to fertilize or sustain plant life."

Omega shrugged. "I know that, but assuming he finds any, he's planning on bringing it back in addition to the specimens we're getting. He says because it's so rare it will be worth a lot on earth. Experts have already speculated we may have to place limits on life expectancy if we're not able to establish housing settlements on this planet. Or future ones, if we live long enough for further exploration."

I could see the angst in his eyes through the protective glass shield of his helmet.

"You're talking about genocide. Who would make the decision to keep searching for phosphorus if it was decided that we needed to decrease the strain on our resources?"

"I don't know," Omega admitted. "He swore me to secrecy, but obviously it's not something I can keep to myself."

I shook my head and went back to work. "That doesn't make any sense. We're on a mission to bring back samples to determine if this place can sustain human life. Mining and bringing back enough phosphate rock to make a substantial impact would take unlimited resources and require a lot of storage space. It would only benefit a few. If they wanted to kill the rest of the population why don't they just put poison in the water, or let us starve and keep everything for themselves?"

"I don't think he is acting on orders from the OWL," Omega replied. "It's possible that he's working with someone else. As it's not part of the mission, he's running a risk by telling me about it."

I stopped my work and leaned against the pick I'd been using to pry a rock sample away, trying to piece together Reynard's actions since we'd left earth. Being secretive about exploring for a mineral that would affect the entire population made me more than suspicious of his motives. My eyes traveled to Omega's. I stared at him for several moments to see if he was holding anything back.

Omega shrugged and glanced away. "All I know is what he told me. I don't know what his ultimate rationale is. Without the right equipment, we can't separate it from the rock, and because of its instability, nor would we want to."

I wasn't convinced. Whatever Reynard was planning it wasn't for the benefit of anyone but Reynard. Of that I was certain.

"Well," I said, "even if we bring phosphate rock back because Reynard ordered us to, we place the entire team in danger by having white phosphorous on board ship. And it's not something we can prepare here and smuggle. We're not equipped for mining. The raw materials will use up the space we need for our samples. Where would we make room to store it?"

"I don't know," he admitted, shaking his head. "You asked me and I told you, but remember," and at that he gave my arm a gentle pull to get my full attention and make the point, "remember you are not to tell anyone that I shared this information."

"What makes you think you're so special? Don't you think that's what he's telling Sig at this very moment?" I retorted.

When Omega's shoulders slumped I knew he hadn't considered that. He believed he was Reynard's sole confidante. I felt certain Reynard was using his 'divide and conquer' strategy again. Not unlike the school bullies who would pull you into their allegiance, then side with your enemies, until everyone was pitted against everyone. I wondered if it was only me who seemed to see that.

"My parents knew Captain Reynard when he was a boy," he said, matter-of-factly. I laughed out loud, pretty sure he was pulling my leg.

"No really," he continued. "I never met him, but my father served with him in the last great war before the OWL took over."

"Was he just as big an asshole back then?"

Omega made a clownish face. "When the OWL recruited me for this mission and my father learned who the leader of the expedition would be, he got really quiet. I asked him if there was a problem. Though he wouldn't say anything specific, probably knowing that speaking out against a fellow officer could result in hard labor, he told me to watch my back. 'The enemy you know is more predictable than the enemy you don't,' he said. I've thought about his words a lot on this trip."

Omega's revelation about Reynard wasn't surprising, but the secret phosphorite mission disturbed me. In the wrong hands it could be used as a way to control population, or eliminate population, especially those who were considered by some as less productive members of society, by limiting distribution to people considered worthy. It had been talked about and discounted even before the formation of the OWL. In fact, though excessive procreation was frowned upon until earth's people had found a new place to colonize, we had not yet resorted to controlling that part of human life.

I arched my back to stretch my aching muscles. I didn't know how much more of this I could take. There was nothing to be done but keep working, and if that meant we dropped in the fields like sharecropping slaves of old, then that was how it had to be. The OWL had issued their ultimatum and I had no choice in the matter. Feeling tired and discouraged, I signaled to the rest of my team and we gathered up our tools and harvested specimens. Then we scrambled onto the Explorer and made our way back to the Astraeus.

There was no one else in sight when we reached the ship. Reynard and Sig had not yet returned. After clearing the airlock and removing my Pangolin suit, I found Rho in the ship's bridge. She whirled around when she heard me come in. After surreptitiously glancing behind me to see if anyone else was nearby, she beckoned to me.

"Come here!" she hissed under her breath. "I need to show you something."

"Can't it wait?" I moaned. "I'm exhausted. I want to clean up and have a drink or tablet of something really inebriating."

"No! Get over here."

I sighed and peeled my clinging bodysuit halfway down, revealing a sweat-sticky T-shirt underneath, and walked over to the console. "What's so important…?"

But as she brought the ship's computer monitor to life there came a crash and then a scream from behind me. I turned and inadvertently let out a gasp.

Reynard was hunched over on his hands and knees, crawling across the floor. A trail of blood followed his movements. Rho leapt from her chair to help him. I dashed past him to the stateroom and grabbed towels and the first-aid kit. Then I ran back to the bridge. Together we half-lifted, half-dragged Reynard as he struggled and swore, onto a reclined chair that would have to serve as an impromptu gurney until we could get him to the sickbay. Rho stood there trying to catch her breath for a few moments, unable to move. Her face had turned the color of sand.

After I surmised she was all right, I turned to Reynard, whom I cared much less about.

"Where's Sig?" I demanded. Reynard groaned and coughed. I gave his shoulders a brutal shaking, not concerned whether it would exacerbate any injuries he might have.

"Where the fuck is Sig?"

Without opening his eyes he said, "He's dead. We were ambushed by something out there. We never saw it coming. It knocked me down and dragged him away. It came at us so fast we never had a chance."

"Did you even look for him?" He gave no answer. I shook him harder. "Reynard, where's Sig's body?" But he moaned again as if in agony and fell into unconsciousness.

Rho reached into the first aid kit and pulled out a clean syringe and a bottle of morphine.

"What are you doing?" I demanded. "He needs to be kept cognizant until we can get more information. We have to figure out where he and Sig were working when they were attacked. If we don't we have no way of finding him out there to bring him back."

She continued to ignore me as she drew out a high dosage of the painkiller. I saw that the dose was strong enough to knock out a very large man, and though tall, Reynard was slender with a medium-sized frame.

"What?" I repeated.

"Shut up," she muttered. "I know what I'm doing. Hold his arm." She tore open a sterile wipe and swabbed his forearm, then injected the needle and continued until the syringe was empty. Then she placed a sticker over top of the injection site.

"We need answers, all right, but we're not going to

get them from him."

"How do you know that?" I demanded. "For certain we're not going to get answers if he's drugged into oblivion. And all hell's going to break loose when he wakes up."

I stared down at Reynard. She'd knocked him out pretty good. Maybe he wouldn't wake up. The thought occurred to me that it wouldn't be such a terrible thing if he didn't. But it might complicate life considerably for the rest of us.

As I glanced at the bleeding Reynard I realized I'd better start attending to his wounds, whatever their nature. The OWL would not look favorably on a team that failed to follow orders or administer assistance to a superior. Rho made no attempt to help. I knew she was thinking the same thing as me: 'If Reynard is here, where is Sig?' But there was no time to speculate on what had taken place. For the moment I was in charge. I turned back to her and gave the order.

"Get the others. Now."

VI

I heard her scream before she came into view. Xi's cries of anguish echoed throughout the ship. "Where is he? Where is he?" She burst into the stateroom and threw herself toward Reynard. "What the fuck have you done with Sig? Why didn't you help him?"

Omega and Chi rushed forward to hold her back while I barricaded her from reaching Reynard. "We don't know and you can't ask him. He's sedated."

Xi ripped herself free of the men's grasp and yelled at me, "Why the hell did you drug him? Now he can't tell us where Sig is."

I turned to Rho. "You'll have to ask Rho."

Rho had adopted a 'take charge' attitude, busying herself by putting away the supplies. She tossed the used syringe into a trash receptacle.

"Reynard said they were attacked. That something dragged Sig off. We need to arm ourselves against whatever it might be and send a search party for Sig." She glanced at each of us in turn.

"Xi, you're too emotional. You're better off staying

here with me. You can help me dress Reynard's wounds. Zeta, I think you and Omega should be the ones to go. I may need Chi here if Reynard wakes up and gives us any trouble."

We all stared at Rho as if she'd gone crazy. But she was dead serious. "Before you leave I want you to help me put Reynard in restraints. When you get back I need to show all of you what I discovered while you were out today. Trust me when I tell you we can't let Reynard out of our sight. But our top priority right now is to find Sig. If he's even alive."

She reached out and touched Xi, who angrily shook her hand away. Rho turned to the rest of us. "Arm yourselves well." She paused for a moment then grabbed the portable first aid kit and handed it to me, giving me a knowing look. I knew what it meant. Handing me the first aid kit was mostly for Xi's benefit. If what Reynard said was true it was unlikely we'd find Sig, either alive or dead.

"Now go!" she ordered, and turned back to administer to Reynard.

Omega whirled around to face Chi and me. Chi looked like he wanted to be anywhere other than going back out to search for Sig and face who knew what that took him. Omega gave him a gentle slap on the arm.

"You stay here and help Rho. It's up to Zeta and me, now. We'll find him." Chi nodded in glum agreement, but I could see he was secretly relieved at not having to accompany us.

Omega and I double checked each other's suits and equipment, then headed toward the airlock. The Pup, the smaller ATV, was still where Reynard had left it after returning from his latest exploration. Omega climbed into the driver's seat and I hopped onto the seat beside him.

Omega steered toward the parked Explorer, the larger vehicle we used to transport ourselves to the sites where we obtained the specimens. It was more difficult to maneuver it around tight spaces, but it was more reliable on the rough terrain.

"We'll make better time and it'll be the only way we could get him back if we find him."

I followed Omega, carrying my pistol in one hand and the first aid kit in the other. My heart thumped so loudly in my chest I felt as if Omega could hear it. It wasn't Sig I was worried about finding, no matter what condition he was in. My biggest concern was what had attacked a man like Reynard. With his Marine training and duration spent in the service, he would never have been taken unaware unless the adversary out there was more skilled, or more dangerous, than he. Or considerably larger. That was as far as I would let my imagination travel.

As we always worked around the clock without any real dark or light on this neon planet, the terrain looked no different now than it did when we had been harvesting the rock, soil, and gas specimens. Omega steered the Explorer over the rocks with skilled caution, its headlights illuminating the blue glow like a surreal fog. I cast a large search beam back and forth along the sides and in our wake. Occasionally we took turns calling out his name. While it was impossible to know what direction Reynard and Sig had traveled, Omega had been with Reynard on earlier exploratory missions. If anyone would know where to begin to look for Sig, it would be Omega.

After nearly an hour of searching and calling out Sig's name, we became weary. If Sig were unharmed and still in his suit and helmet, he could survive the planet's cold and lack of breathable air for an indefinite amount of time. But if it had been compromised in any way, well, we didn't want to think about that. Then there was Reynard's report that they had been attacked. And because we did not know the enemy, we were not prepared for a confrontation with a being that had home advantage.

Omega brought the Explorer to a stop and turned to me. "I'm sorry, Zeta, I think we need to get back to the ship and deal with whatever has happened. If Reynard has regained consciousness he can do more to help us find Sig than we can aimlessly driving around." When I didn't answer, he reached out and patted my knee, and for some reason that didn't upset me.

"I don't want to face Xi without having good news for her." My head dropped in frustration. Or any news, really, good or bad. It had seemed possible to find Sig when we set out, but the landscape was so difficult to maneuver he could be in a thousand places. Or, and this idea I'd tried really hard not to think about, depending on what had taken him he might not even exist other than in some creature's stomach.

Omega started the Explorer and we turned around. Then, as the headlights beam shone across the vast rocky waste, I saw a glint of light. A surge of hope shot through me.

"Over there!" I shouted. "Did you see that?"

Omega put the vehicle into the stationary position. "Where? What did it look like?"

But I had already clambered down from the vehicle and sprinted in the direction of the spurt of light I'd so briefly picked up.

"Zeta!" he shouted. "Wait! For god's sake, don't go off on your own."

I heard him jump from the Explorer and his footsteps as he ran after me, following my tracks and my light. And then I saw what it was that had been illuminated in the vehicles headlights. A strip of the luminous blue Kevlar and spun titanium scales used to make our uniforms dangled from a rocky outcrop like a flag. Beside it lay a helmet. And the symbol Σ that should have been at the front of the helmet had been torn off and was missing. I fell to my knees and gathered the remnants from Sig in my arms. Sobbing, I scarcely noticing when Omega picked me up and carried me back to the Explorer.

Forcing myself to stop crying because it was fogging up my helmet visor, I set the items on the floor of the vehicle and we climbed inside, neither of us speaking as we started our grim voyage back to the Astraeus. The sudden halting of the Explorer almost threw me out of the seat.

"What are you doing?" I demanded of Omega. But he had already gotten out of the vehicle, leaving me sitting there as he picked his way through the rocky outcrops. I stood, trying to see by the beam of light that shone from his helmet exactly what he was so determined to reach. He dropped to the ground then jumped up and turned, waving both his arms in the air as he called out my name.

Avoiding stepping on Sig's items on the Explorer floor, I scrambled from the vehicle. Then I set out after Omega, stumbling as I ran over the rough stony round. When I reached Omega he was tugging on what appeared to be a jagged piece of steel, dulled from age.

"What is that?"

Without identifying marks, the oblong section of steel, nearly a yard long, could have been from anything. A flaking circle of red and yellow paint gave no additional clues. He turned it over and handed it to me so he could see the underside. I fastened my questioning gaze on him.

He shrugged. "I don't know what it is, or what it

could be from, all this way out here. My best guess is that it's space debris from an old satellite."

I frowned, rubbing at the red paint that came away on my glove. "We need to get back to the others at the base and tell them about Sig. Right now we don't have time to look for more related to this piece. If it even has any relevance. It's not like a mission has landed here, or we'd have seen evidence of that already."

Omega glanced around and walked a few more steps in various directions, all the while scanning the area. But it was apparent that this was the only fragment of metal, and as he'd said, was most likely space debris. The solar system was full of spent rocket and satellite trash.

"I'll take it back so we can have a closer look at it," he said, "just in case it turns out to not be something manufactured on earth."

We headed back to the Explorer and climbed inside, the rest of the drive uneventful with each of us lost in our own thoughts. When we reached the encampment, I gathered up what we'd found of Sig while Omega put the Explorer away. After we exited the airlock, we stowed the section of metal in the equipment room. As we helped each other remove our outer gear, we didn't speak. I knew we were thinking the same thing: how we would present Sig's items to Xi. There was nothing to be done but face her and share what we'd discovered.

The scene that met us when we entered the sick-bay was not quite the way we'd left it. Reynard had regained consciousness and his face was purple with barely con-cealed rage. His mouth had been taped shut with duct tape. He fought against his restraints so hard that a trail of broken blood vessels had appeared above his bandages. Omega and I stood there gaping at the rest of the team in dismay. Rho, it appeared, had taken charge.

Omega, as senior in command with Reynard out of commission, would now automatically step up to be our leader. He took a few moments to assess the situation, which was by no means explained by what we were witnessing then addressed Rho.

"What's going on here?"

She glanced to each of us in turn, giving Reynard a look of pure hatred before she replied, "I won't discuss it in front of him. Chi, take him to the stateroom and make sure he's secure then meet us in the bridge."

I snuck a surreptitious glance at Reynard, who would have been frothing at the mouth were it not for the duct tape covering it. I followed Rho into the bridge. Chi, a martial arts enthusiast with formidable muscle structure, would give even Reynard second thoughts about attempting to overpower him. Roughly forcing Reynard to his feet, he gave him a shove in the direction of the corridor that led to the stateroom. Confident Chi would make certain Reynard was well secured, Xi and Omega followed us. Xi rushed forward and grabbed my arm.

"Did you find anything?" I realized then that I'd set Sig's helmet down in the airlock when we'd removed our outer clothing. I had the scrap of material from his suit tucked into my waist pack. It tore at my heart to do it, but I pulled out the fabric and handed it to her without a word. She collapsed into the nearest chair, sobs wrenching her body.

Though I knew everyone felt the same as me, we didn't have the luxury of time to spend consoling each other about Sig. We needed to address the issue of what had happened to two of our crew mates, in spite of our feelings about Reynard. Not to mention, what it had been that attacked them. And most important of all, how would this affect our mission and its outcome.

I turned first to Omega, then to Rho. "What is it you've been trying to tell us?"

She leaned over the ship's main computer console and brought up the communications transmission log. Because of my recent cross training, I also knew how to access the files although I hadn't been working with them since we'd landed. She motioned for us to come forward.

"Tell us what we're looking at," Omega said impatiently. Having finished securing Reynard, Chi crossed the room and joined us at the console.

Rho took a deep breath. "We're supposed to be in communication with the Control Unit Base on a daily basis. That's been Reynard's job to date, to report our progress with the acquisition of specimens from this planet, things that are going well, or not well, projected return, etc. But I haven't been able to find a transmission to CUB since a few weeks after we landed."

Omega frowned. "Are you sure it's not a malfunction? Are all the systems operating properly?"

"I'm sure. Don't you think I'd check and recheck everything before I mentioned it to you? But that's not all." She hesitated, looking distraught, as if uncertain how to continue.

"What else? Wouldn't there be a communication from CUB, especially if they hadn't heard from us in a certain time frame?" Chi asked. He had his arm around Xi; her face swollen and blotched from crying rested against his shoulder.

Rho shook her head. "Not anymore," she said slowly, "because in Reynard's last transmission to CUB he informed them that he had lost his entire crew to alien forces shortly after we'd brought in our first load of samples."

"What!" Omega's fists balled up. He made a move

toward the stateroom as if to deal with Reynard himself, but Chi stepped forward, placing his hands against Omega's chest.

"Wait," said Chi. "We need to figure out what he's been up to and more importantly what his ultimate plan is for us. If he told CUB that we're dead there's nothing to stop him from making that actually happen. Maybe he already did that with Sig."

Rho looked at me and gave a nod. "Tell them." Everyone turned to look at me.

"What do you know?" Omega asked.

I explained to them what had happened during the flight, that Reynard had been awake for most, if not all, of the journey. I told them he hadn't expected me to awaken early, but my personal chemistry had somehow metabolized differently the drugs we'd taken for the flight. So while I was awake and present, he'd had to alter his plans a bit, whatever they were, until he'd been able to complete the setup for his own mission.

"Why would he tell Control that he'd lost his crew?" Xi whispered. "He couldn't have known that he and Sig would be attacked. Unless..." An expression that I couldn't quite fathom crossed her face, but I could see the others were all having the same thoughts as those occurring to me. Perhaps it wasn't outside forces that had attacked Sig. Maybe it was Reynard and he had hidden Sig's body, leaving just enough of his belongings for us to find.

"I still don't understand," Chi said. "Why would he want us gone? He couldn't possibly harvest all the gas and solids samples on his own, especially in such a short space of time. It's been hard enough with six of us." He stopped after seeing Xi's face change. "And now five. It doesn't make sense."

"Not unless he wanted to use the area the crew would take up in the chambers to store extra materials," I said. "Such as phosphorite that Omega told me he's been looking for. He wants all the accolades and money for himself. And he'd get it because we wouldn't be there to collect."

Omega shook his head in disbelief. "But why kill Sig so early when we're still collecting specimens here? An extra set of hands would be able to bring in more results, and the phosphate rock, faster. He wouldn't need to kill any of us until it was just about time to go."

"Maybe Sig knew something. Or figured it out," I said. "He had been going on these explorations with Reynard the most lately. I don't know if anyone else noticed this, but Sig had been acting really strangely around Reynard the last few times they went out. Reynard would have to have told him what to look for, so he would have known about the phosphate rock. Or maybe there was an incident that put his life at risk and Reynard couldn't take the chance of him letting the rest of us know before we'd done all the labor for him."

We all stood quietly, lost in our thoughts and trying to figure out our options. There was no question that failure was not one of them. We had to keep compiling and logging in data; and we had to move on. The only thing now was that we were actually down two sets of hands: Sig's and Reynard's.

"Shouldn't we contact CUB and let them know what has happened?" Xi asked.

Rho threw her a glance weighted with sympathetic sadness, but shook her head.

"Reynard's disengaged something in the transmission equipment. Omega is the only one of us who has the skills to figure out how to fix it. If he can't do it, we're going to have to try and coerce or trick Reynard into repairing it. But if we contact CUB they'll think it was us who mutinied and attacked him. The problem is that now he's bound and gagged we can't take the chance of releasing him. He'll either abandon us or kill us." She shrugged. "Same results either way.

"No," she continued, "here's how I think we should handle things. Because we have no other choice, we'll maintain communications silence until we've finished the mission, and when we're close to leaving we'll try and get Reynard to repair or reconnect the transmission equipment. Then we'll decide what to do with him. We can keep him sedated and secured in the stateroom."

"I think he should suffer the same fate as what he had planned for us," Xi muttered. "Or lock him in his chamber with a lethal dose of curare."

Rho gave a humorless laugh. "That's certainly an option. For now, we have to get to work. And we'll be down one additional person at all times because someone's going to have to guard the bastard." She shot me a look. I nodded.

"I'll take first shift," I volunteered. "I owe it to Sig."

We all disassembled then, the four of them heading to the equipment room to get suited up, and me for the stateroom to guard Reynard. I could see his smirk behind the duct tape and I longed to kick him in the face. It took a Herculean effort to hold myself back. I realized it had been quite a long time since he'd had anything to eat or drink. Not that I gave a damn if he died of starvation, but if we couldn't get the transmission equipment to function on our own we needed to keep him alive.

I brought out a variety of our nutritional food bars and water and set them to one side of him. Then I ripped off the duct tape as roughly as I could. He winced and a tiny crimson bubble formed on his lower lip. I ignored it, grabbing him underneath the jaw, and squeezing until his mouth popped open like a pod. I broke small chunks off the bars and dropped pieces down his throat, pouring water in to wash them down until he choked. I'm not even ashamed to say I enjoyed his discomfort.

"You'll never make it without me," he said between mouthfuls. "You need to keep me alive. You don't have the experience or training to commandeer this ship back to earth. There isn't one of you who possess the skills or knowledge necessary if you encounter hostile forces."

"You mean like you?" I said with a laugh. I was in the middle of getting ready to give him another drink and instead poured it down his neck.

"Hey!" he yelled, squirming. "Have some respect. You're not even twenty-one rotations yet."

I reattached a new piece of duct tape over the lower half of his face, collected the dishes and wrappers and straightened up. Then I gave him a sharp kick in the groin with the toe of my boot.

"Whoops, sorry, I slipped," I said gaily, smiling as he jerked and jackknifed, his scream of pain muffled behind the duct tape.

"Haven't you heard, bitch?" I said. "Twenty-one is the new forty." Then I settled down into a comfortable chair and left him to his private agony while I sat and watched him writhe.

VII

T-46

We stepped up the production of harvesting specimens to a pace that would have made Reynard proud, which was not what we wanted, but what we needed to do. There was no further talk of phosphorite or even Sig, there were just our collective efforts to complete the mission and return home to earth in the allotted time. Through Reynard, CUB had been alerted that he would be the only member of the team returning with a cargo hold of all the samples and specimens, and possibly even the phosphorous. Though how many people with the OWL or at the CUB were aware of the parallel mission Reynard was engaged in was still a mystery. Our return plans were the reverse of what CUB knew. The team was all of the same mind and in complete agreement on one thing: Reynard would not be returning home with us as captain of the mission.

We slept for two hours at a time. Sleep became a luxury that we took in shifts so as to keep working around the clock. The rest of the time we alternated the labor of acquiring specimens, analyzing and labeling them, and logging our findings into the computer. The strain was apparent in our work and our tempers, but we kept on. We still needed to keep a guard on Reynard at all times. And the only person spared from guard duty was Xi, for obvious reasons.

Chi and I worked as a team on the harvest, while Omega and Xi did the testing and labeling. Rho was in the ship guarding Reynard, a task she'd been looking forward to. I didn't need to caution her about him; she'd been the first to discover his treachery and wouldn't readily give him an opportunity to escape.

Chi straightened up from his crouching position where he'd been scraping bits off the rock face. He stretched then glanced at me. "I think we should put Reynard to work. He's useless in there. We're wasting having an extra able bodied person at all times just guarding him. Any one of us could just as easily be guarding him while he's collecting samples."

He had a point. Our problem was that Reynard was a former combat Marine. If he wasn't shackled properly he could be deadly, even for someone with skills like Chi's. He could single out or overtake any of us, systematically killing one by one until everyone was gone. Then he could complete the mission on his own as best he could. He'd already told CUB that we were dead. It wasn't as if he would need to change his story.

As I considered what Chi said, I scratched without purpose at an outcropping of rock. "Whoever is guarding him while he works would have to be armed with the weapon pointed at him at all times. Not to mention, he'd have to be shackled just in case he tried to make a break for it."

He nodded. "I've given it a lot of thought and I believe it can work. He's strong, he's healthy; he will be better rested than all of the rest of us put together. At the very least it might get us back on track so we can leave Planet Hell ahead of schedule."

Planet Hell. That's what it had become to us. We'd changed the name from Planet A, or Planet Hope, as we'd called it in the past. With its unchanging landscape, neither day nor night, no seasons or habitation, at least none that we knew of, it was as close to a living Hell as any of us had ever known. Hopefully would ever know.

"Let's talk to the others about it," I said. "I think it is a terrific idea. Dibs on being the first to put him to work."

Chi burst into laughter. "You won't get an argument from me."

Xi and Omega were all for it. Rho wasn't so sure.

"While it's a good plan in theory," she said, "I've got a bad feeling about this. He's tricky and he fights dirty. And he has absolutely no qualms about seeing that we all die, as that's been his intent all along." She gave us all a pointed look. "It makes me very, very nervous having him out there with us, even if he is shackled and at gunpoint."

"I love the idea," Xi said, not even bothering to soften the furious hatred in her voice. In the days since Sig's disappearance, deep lines had formed on her face, aging her beyond her nineteen rotations. "Let me take the first slave-shift."

Chi gave her a sympathetic smile. "Sorry, sweetie," he said. "We're not letting you anywhere near him with a gun. He'll get his dues, but we might as well get the work out of him before we use him up."

Xi's dark eyes glowered under their hooded lids, but

didn't respond.

"I'll take first shift," Omega said. "I'm the oldest and more or less expected to be in charge now. We might as well see how it's going to work with me in charge of putting him to work before letting the rest of you deal with him. Remember, I've accompanied him during his explorations, so I know how he operates."

"Okay," said Rho. "Let's get to our stations and you can put him to work during your next shift. Omega, why don't you take an extra hour of sleep so you'll be alert." She gave him a meaningful look before turning to address the rest of us.

"For god's sake, no one is to tell him what we're doing or engage him in any conversation. He'll twist and turn whatever you say. The duct tape remains on his mouth at all times unless someone is feeding him. Agreed?"

And we all agreed because we knew what the consequences would be if Reynard were allowed to get free.

VIII

T-35

Our utilization of Reynard as slave-labor material was a stroke of brilliance on Chi's part. It gave us immense satisfaction to be calling the shots, determining how many hours he'd work and when to let him rest. In fact, we became more exhausted just supervising him and finding menial grunt work for him to do once the heavy labor was completed than he did performing the tasks. It occurred to me that if he'd been assisting all along with the regular harvest of the planet's specimens that we'd have almost completed our mission by now. But of course, we still had a long way to go, and less than a month to do it in, if you took the span to make the voyage back into consideration.

Xi had gradually come to terms with Sig's disappearance, though she never failed to cast daggers of sheer hatred toward Reynard whenever they were in the same vicinity. He gave no indication of any malice toward her because of it, although it was his fault, if not directly, then indirectly, that Sig had died. He was the officer in charge; he was responsible.

I listened in one night from the anonymity of the bridge, in a rare moment when Omega had Reynard's gag removed while he ate in the common area. Chi and Xi were out in the field, so I wasn't worried they would hear anything. Omega's voice was muted but Reynard's drill sergeant tones rose loud and clear through the walls.

"I didn't kill Sig," he was saying. "I don't know what took him because it came at us from behind. There's something out there besides us and we need to be prepared should it come around again."

Then I heard Omega's voice. "None of us believe you. We found your transmission to CUB that informed them we'd all died. Zeta told us that you were awake for days, if not the whole time, while we were in flight. What's your explanation for that?"

The silence that ensued was so long I wondered if they'd moved from the common area to the rear of the ship. Finally Reynard spoke again, apparently choosing to not answer Omega's question.

"Are you planning to leave me here once the harvest is complete?"

"We haven't decided what we're going to do with you," Omega said. At that point I was beginning to think that Omega was sharing too much information with Reynard, especially what we knew and didn't know. I nonchalantly entered the room as if I hadn't overheard anything. They both glanced at me in surprise.

"Bonjour, blancmange," said Reynard with a sneer, "what brings you to the bistro?"

I ignored him, though my first instinct was to snap back at him. I'd bide my time until we were alone. I moved over to Omega and patted him on the shoulder.

"If he's finished his meal, I'll take over for the next shift."

Omega nodded and picked up the food containers, heading to the sterilization unit. "He's worked a full six hours already. He should probably be allowed to rest now."

I spun around and hissed at him, "I don't give a fuck if he's worked twenty-four hours. He's working for me now."

Omega backed out of the room with a mixture of concern and alarm clouding his face. Reynard's eyes followed his exit then he laughed out loud, which was a mistake. I reached for the duct tape, ripped off a strip and slapped it across his mouth, causing him to reel back in pain. Then I grabbed what there was of his hair and jerked his head back so he would be forced to look at me.

"Now there's no question that you are one devious motherfucker," I said. "But there's something you should remember: never fuck with someone who's got nothing to lose. Now get your traitorous ass up and get back to work."

He rolled his eyes at me in an exaggerated fashion and it took all the restraint in my body to keep from kicking him in the groin again. I called Omega back into the equipment room to help me get Reynard suited up for outside while I did put on my own. After we were readied we headed for the airlock.

Once outside, I handcuffed Reynard to the Explorer and put shackles on his ankles. Then we set off for Sector 6, the latest harvest area. There we met Xi and Chi just returning from their shift. Xi kept her gaze averted to avoid looking at Reynard, but Chi gave him a big sarcastic grin. Rho was still out at work and we would be joining her for a few hours until her shift was up and Omega would arrive after his rest.

I pushed Reynard in the direction of the equipment and unfastened the cuffs from his hands, but I left his legs in shackles. I kept my gun out of its holster whenever I was in charge of him, though I had it on safety. It gave me a small measure of security that I wouldn't hesitate to use lethal force should he try to overcome me.

Rho straightened up when she saw us and headed over.

"How's he working today?" she asked. "Doing his share? He was a lazy son-of-a-bitch yesterday." She giggled. We always said something along those lines, whether he worked hard or slacked off. Just to put a semblance of humor into our otherwise hard, colorless lives. I myself was beginning to feel jaded and tough, which at the age of nineteen was not a desirable trait. In fact, it had been my birthday two weeks earlier and I hadn't even thought about it until it was long past. Life at the present was not a joyous event for any of us.

"He's getting a bit cocky again." I could see from his stance, even when he was working, that he listened intently. I lowered my voice. "I think that everyone who is assigned to watching him needs an extra hour of sleep just to be on their toes," I said. "We can't trust him an inch. And if he gets free, even if he doesn't kill us, he'll likely take the ship and leave us stranded."

She nodded. "I think you're right." She gave my arm a nudge. "Hey, my shift is almost up. Do you think you'll be all right here with him until Omega comes back? I haven't eaten in hours and I'm starting to get hypoglycemic."

"I'm good," I said. "Omega had plans to rest for a while, but it would be safer if I wasn't alone with the asshole. Radio Omega and tell him to get out here fast."

Rho gave me a slight hug with one arm and through

her visor I saw her wink. Then she climbed into the Pup ATV and headed off toward the ship. As soon as she was out of sight, Reynard stood. I felt a surge of adrenaline, knowing he could overpower me if I didn't keep a certain amount of distance between us.

"Get back to work," I said. "I'm watching every move you make and it would be nothing to me to blow your damned kneecaps out. You could still harvest specimens lying on your belly."

He raised his arms in an exaggerated plea and went back to work. But not before giving me a sly glare. There was more in his eyes than I'd wanted to see, and I knew what it was. He was thinking I was turning into him. But he'd also figured out by now that I was no one to mess with.

I suppressed a sigh so he couldn't tell how physically and emotionally exhausted I'd become. We were close to our goal, but we were also close to screwing up because of keeping to our schedule and having to watch Reynard every second. If it hadn't been for our system to check and double check each other's work and sample harvest logs, we'd have messed up significantly several times already.

Out of habit I checked my gun, making sure all the chambers were full. It was our standard issue laser shot pistol, with a large enough caliber to take out a rhinoceros if we hit it dead on between the eyes. Not that we were expecting anything like that out here, but there were too many unknowns for my liking and we still had questions. Especially after the attack on Sig and Reynard.

A rustling noise from some distance behind me caused me to half-turn. Omega should be arriving at any moment, but he'd be on the Pup ATV that Rho had just returned to the Astraeus on, the one we used to shuttle back and forth. This left the crew that remained working in the vulnerable situation of having only the larger Explorer, which was laden with specimens and so only moved when it became full. Which also made it slow and heavy. Without the smaller ATV we didn't have transportation until the next shift arrived. It wasn't the most perfect system, but it was what we had to make do with, being under equipped in so many ways.

But neither Omega, nor the Pup ATV, were anywhere in sight. In any case, he would be coming from the direction opposite the sound. A smell of something nasty and unfamiliar wafted over to me. I glanced at Reynard, who appeared not to have heard or noticed anything and worked diligently at the specimen logging station. I made a mental note to have one of the male crew supervise his hygiene habits. Fortunately for us, Reynard knew all our jobs and there wasn't much he couldn't do. And of course, the main reason he was still alive was because he had yet to repair the ship's communication system before we could leave the planet.

Then came another sound, and this one Reynard heard. He jackknifed to attention, and even with the visor in place I could make out that his face had gone dead white. My stomach did a flip-flop. I'd never seen him react in any way other than authority or defiance. Certainly not apprehension, let alone fear. He glanced at me and made motions with his hands, indicating for me to remove the duct tape from underneath his helmet. I wouldn't have been able to even if I'd wanted because by doing so I'd expose him to the unbreathable atmosphere. I waved the gun at him.

"You're keeping that on," I said. "There's nothing out here, just some of the equipment shifting. Get back to work."

He hesitated a few moments then did as he was told, but all the while his eyes were wary. He glanced around our surroundings once more, shook his head and went back to his task. I swallowed hard, unnerved by his apprehension, and put my attention on high alert for any unfamiliar noise. Not taking my eyes off him, I pulled my radio communicator off my belt.

"Omega, if you can hear this, give me your location."

No response came back on the device. I made the transmission again, and still there was no answer. Reynard ceased working and stood there watching me, no doubt waiting for me to make a mistake or have my attention distracted so he could run for the Explorer and leave me stranded. Keeping him in my line of sight prepared me for almost anything. But then my peripheral vision caught a movement that wasn't Reynard or Omega. Without warning, everything went black.

When I regained consciousness the first thing I noticed was an ungodly smell; a rancid and rotten stench like that of decomposing flesh. Involuntarily I gagged, but managed to keep from vomiting, which would have been unbearable trapped inside my helmet. By what stroke of luck I still had my helmet, I couldn't say, though it obscured my vision somewhat. A dank darkness made it impossible to identify my surroundings. Though my back and the calves of my legs burned, it wasn't the pain that comes from broken bones. But they ached like nothing I'd felt before and it was only then that I realized I was lying on my stomach with my arms and legs hogtied. Spots blurred my vision from hyperventilating. I tried to retrace my last thoughts against the rising panic, willing myself to take slow, deep breaths. How long had I'd been unconscious?

I'd been keeping watch on Reynard and calling

Omega on the communicator as we were never to be working alone, especially if we were supervising Reynard. I must have been ambushed from behind. Something had been hiding in the low rocky outcrops and Reynard had heard it before it attacked. But where was Reynard? Had he managed to get away? Or, even though I'd watched him carefully, was it possible I been attacked by Reynard?

I wriggled my feet and hands, trying not to make any noise while I attempted to loosen my bonds. Whatever or whoever had snatched me was most likely very close, and their plans for my future probably weren't in my favor. If it was Reynard it wouldn't make any difference if I talked to him. He could ignore me or not.

"Reynard," I hissed. "Where the fuck are you?"

For several minutes my words were followed by only an ominous silence. Then I heard a groan, a human sound, not far away.

"Reynard, are you tied up, too? Or was it you who attacked me, you motherfucker?"

The moan came again and along with the smell of sheer nastiness came something else that I recognized. The hot metallic odor of fresh blood.

"Are you hurt?"

"Shut the fuck up," Reynard whispered. "If they hear us they'll come back. Yes, I'm hurt. If they don't finish us off, I'll live. But I wouldn't count on that."

"What are they?"

There was such a long silence that I thought he'd either fallen asleep or died. Finally he said, "I don't know. I've never gotten a good look at them, not even when they took Sig."

My head shot up so fast I wrenched my back. "What do you mean, they took Sig?"

"Sorry to disappoint you and change your opinion of

me, but I told the truth. Sig and I were attacked. I managed to roll under a rocky ledge and they couldn't find me. I don't know what they are or what they want with us." He went silent for a few moments and then I heard a scraping noise, the sound of something moving toward us.

"Be quiet and pretend you're still unconscious," Reynard whispered. "It might be your only chance."

Along with the sound of the unknown creature entering the area where we lay came that terrible smell again. It was nearly impossible to be quiet and not retch, so I breathed as shallowly as I could, still unable to raise my head to see. Whatever created the stench had to be terrible enough to permeate the helmet filters.

The thing shuffled and dragged itself along, no lithe or sudden movements there. It stopped short of me, in the direction of where Reynard's voice came from. I heard a thump, then another, and on the third louder thump, a yelp of pain from Reynard. I realized it must be either pounding or kicking him. There was nothing I could do, even if I could see them. I held my breath waiting for my turn, and bracing myself for more pain.

Then came the sound of a large object being dragged and as it bumped past me I saw in shadows that it was Reynard being hauled away, though what pulled him along was still shrouded in the darkness. I didn't know if Reynard was unconscious now from the beating, or faking, or dead. Obviously faking would result in getting beaten less so I stayed as quiet as I could, fearful to make any motion at all.

I'd managed to roll onto my side when the thing returned without Reynard. I'd kept my eyes closed but I needed to see the enemy, if the dimness would allow. The darkness filled the area around me, but less in the direction that it had taken Reynard. It appeared now that I was in some sort of cave, with a blue neon glow illuminating the creature from behind. And then I got a good look at it.

Though it walked on two lower legs, it had two upper legs that hung nearly to the knees. An enormous head of sorts jutted out of the top. The entire body was bluish, lumpy and misshapen, with weeping ulcerations and patches of scabs and yellowish hair covering the surface. Though the arms bent and moved in humanoid fashion, the tips of the hands ended in blackened stumps, without the benefit of fingers. Now I recognized the smell. It was that of gangrenous flesh.

The creature assumed a crouch a few feet away and stared at me with two eyes sunken behind pustulent sores in its featureless blue-grey face. It appeared to have no difficulty breathing the planet's atmosphere. When it made no further moves, I decided to see if I could communicate with it.

"What do you want with me?" I asked it in a low calm tone, so as not to alarm it. "Why haven't you killed me?"

It stared at me in curiosity then opened its mouth. I nearly lost my previous meal. It had several rows of rotten teeth and the smell from within its body was ten times worse than the exterior. It made a low guttural sound and the foulness of its breath nearly felled me. One of its teeth dropped to the ground. It busied itself stirring around in the dirt with its paw until it found the tooth. Struggling to grasp it in its palm it eventually managed to thrust the ochre lump back into its reeking maw.

"Would you untie me?" It just stared back, then eventually made a rollicking movement that I realized was the only way it was able to rise properly as it had no digits on its feet for stability. I made a mental note that this seemed to be at least one of its weaknesses. It had a bad sense of balance. But evidenced at how it was able to drag both Reynard and me without much effort, it was also much stronger than me. It left me lying there and headed off outside of the cave.

I wondered what it had done with Reynard. Assuming he was alive, we were on the same side now. But if he were dead I was on my own. I worked at what appeared to be woven vines that tied my hands and feet together, twisting and rolling my arms until I had my hands free. Then I was able to untie my feet. I could smell the rot of the creature's flesh where it had rubbed on my bindings and wondered how it was able to fasten anything with those blackened stumps. Then I realized it probably incorporated its teeth, loose as they were, as tools.

Once I was free I concentrated on how to escape. If there were more than one of these creatures I was probably doomed. But if that was the only one my chances were pretty good. For a moment I considered saving my own skin and leaving Reynard. But if he were alive, and was able to make it back to the Astraeus on his own two feet, I could use his help. Or use him as a decoy. I also wasn't so cold hearted as to abandon him to this fate, whatever it might be.

I felt around my body for any of my tools, but it seemed that they'd either fallen off when I was hauled away, or the creature had taken them. My utility belt was still slung around my waist, but gone was my gun and communicator. Feeling deeper into my belt, much to my delight I found a jack knife. That would come in handy. If at some point when I'd escaped and I needed light I still had the beam on my helmet. Carefully I crawled to the darker shadows of the cave to orient myself as to my whereabouts. And then in the dim shadows I saw it.

On top of a neatly folded pile of luminous titanium cloth lay the metallic gold, Greek symbol Σ. Beside the fabric someone had staged a set of two human hands and two feet, almost as if the person to whom they'd belonged had been vaporized away from them. They were shriveled, blackened and partially mummified. A shiny object stood out from the decayed flesh. I crept toward it to take a closer look and saw a ring. Then I realized what I was looking at. It was all that was left of Sig.

I choked back a scream and scrambled backwards, away from the horror of it. The carefully placed items appeared to be some kind of a makeshift shrine, or grave, and it tore my guts apart to think of the rest of Sig's remains.

As I regained my composure, I contemplated my captor. Was the creature an attacker or rescuer? And if it was a rescuer, what could be out there that was worse?

IX

After I'd recovered from discovering what remained of Sig, I evaluated my surroundings and my ability to escape. The shallow cave was just large enough to shelter me, but if the shrine was any indication, it appeared to be only for temporary use, and not for permanent shelter. If I found Reynard and could rescue him, fine, but if he was beyond help then I would get out alone. By now my team would be wondering where we were. And if they sent out a search party they would not be prepared for the creature that had me.

Venturing slowly out, I maintained a crouch position. As I left the cave I straightened up, wincing from being in a cramped position for so long, aching from the scrapes and bruises I'd sustained. There was no evidence anywhere of either the creature or Reynard. This puzzled me. Why would it leave me completely alone and unguarded? Surely it must anticipate an escape attempt at some point. Even the most primitive of creatures staged inescapable traps for their prey.

Certain nothing was watching I tried to determine in

which direction our encampment lay. Without sunlight or the moon to establish a sense of place, all I could do was look to the stars for guidance. But these stars were not of my galaxy. The constellations were as unfamiliar as the nature of my captor, and provided no help.

I examined the ground for signs of scrape marks from us being dragged to see if it made a trail back to where we'd been snatched. But the terrain was so rough and rocky that nothing was displaced or disturbed. And then I saw a shimmer that I recognized, and as I approached I saw that it was pieces of shredded scales from our suit material. Possibly Reynard's, though perhaps Sig's. At least I now had a semblance of a trail to follow.

And then I realized why the creature had been confident enough in my inability to escape that it left me alone. I was in some sort of a compound, with at least 20 foot high, unclimbable walls created out of the very rocks on which I walked. It was a fortress from which I could not immediately discern an exit. A sense of panic overcame me for a moment, but I fought it down. If it could get me in here, then there had to be a way out. And I could find it. I just needed to remain unseen and aware of my surroundings.

Keeping low, I crept on my hands and knees to the rock wall and examined it with the tips of my fingers for a way to climb out. I realized that climbing would be an inconvenience for most creatures, especially if they were carrying prey, so I searched for evidence of a gate. The entire enclosure appeared to be several hundred feet in diameter, but inside there was no indication of dwellings. I thought about that for a few moments and then it dawned on me why that would be. The creature most likely lived underground, perhaps in a cave similar, and larger, than the one I'd been in. And if it was lurking below the surface, I might very well be walking on its roof.

The dim blue neon glow made the entire landscape an even playing surface. No recesses or crevasses stood out in any way. If this was a compound that provided their housing, it was the deadest place I'd ever seen. Then I saw a different color gleaming from the opposite end of the compound. This glow stood out from the blue because it radiated pink. I knew that this was most likely phosphorite, the mineral essential to all life that Reynard had been seeking to bring back to earth. I ventured cautiously toward it.

When I reached the pink light I saw that it emanated from a hole extending from underneath the rock wall, making it appear to be a low archway. I dropped back down to my knees and peered underneath the rocks. A narrow tunnel, scarcely large enough for me to crawl through in a crouch, extended interminably, and though the pink light continued throughout, I couldn't see where it ended. If I tried to use this as a method of escape I could be trapped from either side. On the other hand, if I didn't try I might never get out.

Still on my knees, I felt my way along, all the while looking for a variation in the depth of light. For the longest while I crawled in a void that gave me no sense of getting anywhere, and I forced myself to ignore the pain seeping through my joints. Then I realized that the nature of the glow had changed somewhat, like the color spectrum of a rainbow where it decreases in intensity and blends into another hue. I was now getting into a greenish glow that deepened as I crawled into it. I turned around as much as the limited headroom of the tunnel would allow and saw behind me that the direction from where I'd begun was definitely pinker. I appeared to be making progress, but as to whether it was of a positive or negative nature, I hadn't a clue.

The deeper the green hue became, the wider the opening in the tunnel grew. As it turned out, I was not actually traveling in an escape tunnel, I had been crawling through the entrance to the creature's habitat. I was well underground, and the area was large enough now to the point where I could stand instead of crawl. As I stood I became bathed in the deep multi-hued shades of blue-green. Instead of the rocky, barren outcrops covering the surface of Arianrhod that we were familiar with, all around me were leafy green plants and vegetation. I knew if green were present, there would be chlorophyll. And there would be phosphorous. But most importantly, there would be oxygen.

I stared open mouthed, trying to fathom my surroundings. It was an enormous, expansive area, like a planetarium in an underground greenhouse. The dampness was palpable. Moisture dripped from the rock wall and ceiling surfaces. I could feel condensation building up in my helmet and even my breathable suit was clammy against my skin. The thought, 'the greenhouse effect,' came to me. Something that looked a lot like a tiny lizard skittered past, startling me. I gritted my teeth hard to keep from making any sudden noise that would give me away.

Far off in the distance were two large, moving shapes. The creatures, looking much like the one that had dragged away Reynard, ambled back and forth through what appeared to be a garden. I huddled back against the wall I'd just exited and behind the fronds of some kind of leafy bush. I knew that with my silvery blue suit I stood out like a beacon and sooner or later I'd be detected.

I realized then that it was possible the air here was breathable to me, that it contained enough oxygen to sustain life. Then again, it might not, and I couldn't take the risk of removing my mask or my suit. I watched the creatures move slowly; their halting gait as they stumbled on their blackened feet was painful to see. A rush of sadness came over me. They were piteous, and unless I was mistaken, not something to be feared.

I slouched back against the wall and rested. I would neither confront them nor run away. I would simply stay where I sat until I was discovered and then they could determine my fate. My best chances of survival lay in befriending them and perhaps whatever it was they ate would also be suitable for me. Unless it was me. The thought of the creature's teeth and hygiene made me shudder in disgust.

Time slipped away from me. I don't know how long I'd been there before one of the creatures stumbled toward the long tunnel from which I'd emerged. Very likely it was on its way to where I'd been left and it would be inevitable for it to see me there. I sat quietly as it approached, but stayed down low so as not to appear confrontational. Then it noticed my presence and let out a scream that shattered the air. The idea that I was not in danger disappeared like fog in sunlight.

The second of the things scrambled toward me, semi-upright, in a crouching, apelike run. It was hideously deformed and decaying. Dying, I realized suddenly. They were dying. But their death was a slow, hideous one like that suffered by lepers in leper colonies. Shunned by society and left to die.

They stood in front of me, shrieking and gesticulating. With every movement the smell of decay emanating from them became almost overpowering. I was terrified to the point of blacking out, but forced myself to remain calm. My survival was dependent upon it. Finally I willed myself to speak.

"My name is Zeta. I came here on a mission from earth to harvest samples of the terrain from your planet. If you let me go, my team and I will leave and not return." It was a bold statement, and obviously not one I'd be able to follow through on, given our mission. Still, it sounded plausible to my ears.

But stead of calming them, more wild shrieking followed. Then I realized that they weren't threatening me, they were offering a kind of welcome. The smaller of the two shuffled a short distance away, but the more upright specimen ventured forward. It reached out and without warning the stump of its hand grabbed my helmet and jerked it off. I yelled out in alarm and jumped away from it. My breath came out in a gasp as I fully expected to immediately suffocate from lack of breathable air. Tentatively, I took a shallow breath. An overwhelming sense of well-being came over me. I could breathe the atmosphere. I laughed out loud in relief.

Immediately they shrank back away from me. The silence was so profound that I could hear my own heart. And then I saw the most amazing sight. The smaller of the creatures had tears rolling down its hideous face. Then the two moved together and flanked me, ushering me closer to where they had been working. I now saw that they had no need of shelter as they were in fact, underground, with areas that looked to be where they bedded down at night. Large, nest-like contraptions large enough to hold them and keep them together for warmth were set in tidy clusters within honeycomb type structures.

With the recent commotion, another creature appeared and joined the other two. They urged me forward, none making an attempt to touch me (for which I was thankful), and eventually brought me to another nest.

This new creature was more debilitated, even more decayed than the rest, if that was possible. Its stench was indescribable, but there was something humanistic about it that gave me a sense of kinship. Patches of long grey hairs clung precariously to its sore-covered body, the skin of which was so blue that it became blackened at every tip. It peered at me through clouded eyes and made a grunting sound.

Immediately the smaller creature, which I presumed was the youngest, shuffled off to an area covered with fronds that looked like a makeshift hut. It disappeared inside and was gone for several minutes. When it emerged it bore an armload of items I couldn't quite make out. Then it moved forward in that curious, rollicking gait, and dropped them at my feet. I glanced at the leader. It gave a slow nod and a gesture of its head that indicated I was to look at the items.

I crouched down and examined what had been set before me. In the heap was a pile of ragged khaki cloth that once may have been clothing, a tattered book, a rectangular item made from a substance I hadn't seen in rotations, I believe they called it plastic when it was used more than a half a decade earlier, and what appeared to be an old wooden bowling pin or a large, child's rattle.

I examined the rattle, which was put together in two halves with a top and bottom, segmented in the middle. The painted exterior had long ago weathered and peeled off so as to make it impossible to identify any artwork. I twisted the two halves then slipped them apart. An identical rattle, though smaller, fell to the ground. The paint had been protected on the insert. What I'd thought was a rattle was instead a carved wooden doll with the traditional garb of the ancient country of Russia painted on the surface.

A collective moaning and chortling took up around me. I pulled the second doll apart, and the same thing happened with yet another one inside. I kept doing this until I had six identical, nesting dolls that gradually decreased in size, lying on the ground before me. Not knowing what to make of that, I reassembled them all until there was just the original left. When I stole a look at my captors their faces held a beatific joy I'd never before seen on any creature.

Then I picked up the book. It was covered with a strange writing that was vaguely familiar, but at that moment I couldn't place it. Curious shapes and letters, though not of English origin, and there was nothing of it I could decipher or read. Carefully lifting one crumbling page after another I discovered schematic diagrams of an aircraft, engines, wiring, lighting, not that dissimilar from manuals we had in the ship. Puzzled, I set it back down.

The plastic item was even stranger. It had several buttons and dials, most of which were broken. There was one, though, that was left intact. I pressed it inward and a whirring noise started, then a scratchy, warbling piece of classical music from the Alexander Borodin opera "Prince Igor" began to play. Suddenly the fragile tape inside snapped, and the music ended with a squeal and whirring until I pushed the button again.

It was only then that I realized these beings must be human. Like me, yet not like me.

"Who are you?" I looked around at them all, misshapen, decaying relics and descendants of an earlier mission from some country that existed long before the OWL had taken control of earth.

"I think I can answer that." My heart nearly stopped. But the creatures didn't appear alarmed when Reynard stepped out from the hut, limping heavily, though not bound in any way. I stared at him, dumbfounded. Like me, he wasn't wearing his helmet, and his suit, though torn, appeared relatively intact.

"What is this place?" I said, waving my hand to encompass the creatures, "who are these…what are these?"

He smiled; his usual sardonic demeanor appeared to have returned now he wasn't bound. "Be careful. Some of them can understand a little of what you say. From what I'm able to figure out, they're the lost Cosmonauts, a Russian mission sent out into space in the late 1950's." The three poor creatures gathered around us, the most animated I'd seen any of them, and listened intently.

I shook my head. "We learned about those hoaxes in history classes. They were dismissed, just as the original so-called lunar landings were determined to be hoaxes to show we'd beaten the Soviets in outer space exploration."

Reynard just stared at me. "So, whose hoax do you believe or disbelieve? Are they all lies or was someone telling the truth?"

I didn't have an answer to that so I deflected to another question. "How did they end up here? Even if what you say is true, that the Russians were actually able to enter outer space back then, this galaxy is much farther away than just a lunar landing, or orbiting the earth. There's no way that the ships built in those days could make such a journey. Nor could the crew live the duration it would take to get here. And they would never have been properly equipped to live once they landed."

"I don't have an explanation for how they got here or how they've survived," he said. "If we can communicate with them they might be able to tell us. How's your Russian these days?"

I ignored that. The Russian language, just as all the others, had been abolished for many rotations, long before the OWL's inception. Anyone discovered speaking anything but English would receive a prison sentence. One people, one language, one world. That was the OWL's mantra.

"Are these their descendants?"

Reynard shrugged. "I don't know. One appears younger, and I don't remember if women were on that flight. Or how they would survive childbirth in a place such as this. One thing I can tell you though, my dear."

He leaned close and gave me an evil look fraught with meaning. "They are VERY interested in you. And the other females in our team."

X

Though the creatures hadn't given me any indication they were considering me for breeding purposes, the thought of them touching me in any way was so repugnant as to be unthinkable. When Reynard had dropped his bomb he seemed almost smug about it. Whatever else he knew, he wasn't giving me the whole story. And as I spoke no Russian, or even a fragment of any Cyrillic language, for now I had little hope of communicating with them for anything but the most rudimentary things, such as food.

I wondered what sort of turmoil my team would be experiencing, not only losing Reynard and me, but by now being down to only three people to try and get what they needed before they had to leave the planet. Were they searching for us, I wondered, or had they just assumed we'd fallen victim to the same fate as Sig?

"You realize that you represent survival to them," Reynard remarked. We sat together, untethered and basically free to roam the compound. They knew we were no threat; we had been relieved of our weapons and physically were much smaller than they, not only in stature but in numbers.

"How do you figure that?"

"Depending on how they are looking at you, either for reproduction, or for a means to get off this planet. No matter what, you are the ticket. They saw that I was your prisoner; therefore in their estimation you must be the leader. They no longer possess the strength, knowledge or technology to leave this planet on their own."

I considered this. At that moment, one of the creatures (I thought of it as that because I had yet to think of them as fully human), brought us food and drink. There were cups carved out of rock or clay, filled with what appeared to be water, and the food consisted of a green leafy paste with strips of leathery looking meat. Whatever it was, despite my hunger, it looked as unappetizing as they did. I glanced at Reynard. He had picked up a piece of the meat and sniffed it.

"What do you think it is?" I asked.

He shrugged. "It's either lizard or Sig."

I leaned to one side, bent over and threw up. He laughed at me.

"You're still very young, Zeta," he said. "And that will be your downfall. If you are going to survive this ordeal you are going to have to take what comes and deal with it. If it means they feed you the filet of a former teammate, well then don't offend them. Eat it." He sniffed the meat again. "Actually, it smells more like lizard." He took a bite. "Hmmm, tastes like chicken."

That angered me more than just about anything else he'd ever said or done. But he was a survivor and I could learn from him. I picked up the green leafy material and inhaled the gamey scent, then touched it with my tongue. It tasted kind of like a bitter version of spinach, which would mean it was high in iron, and I could skip the meat. I gobbled it down, giving Reynard as mean a glare as I could muster.

He just laughed. "You'll need the protein sooner or later." Then he took another mouthful and chewed with exaggerated gusto at my nauseated face.

I took a drink from the cup they'd given me. The water was rich in minerals, leaving a tannic taste in my mouth. But I recognized it as being beneficial, like an energy drink. I wondered about their longevity. Could these people really be some of the original Cosmonauts? If so, that would mean that they were well over 100, maybe even 150 rotations old. How had they survived? What would have kept them alive that long?

I remembered from history classes that there had been tribes of Russians who had lived well past a century, but that had been discounted due to lack of record keeping. Still, with every rumor or legend lay a grain of truth. Did these people possess a super gene that we did not? Something extraordinary had kept them alive, given the adverse conditions that they had been subjected to for more than a century.

That they had not made an attempt to molest me also gave me a sense of superiority. Did they have a certain reverence toward me? Or women in general? These people, or their predecessors, had once been the hope of their country. They weren't laborers or laundresses, they had been engineers, scientists, and astronauts of the highest caliber. They spoke the scientific language in which I'd been trained, though we were from completely different backgrounds. This, too, gave me hope. Reynard was still everyone's prisoner. I vowed this would not change. Not if I had anything to do with it.

XI

Until I found a way to communicate at a higher level with the Cosmonauts, as I'd taken to calling them, I kept contact with them to a minimum. They approached me with food and water, and I, in turn, studied their book. When I understood enough I would attempt a discussion with their leader, find out what it was they planned to do with me and my team. Despite what Reynard said, I wasn't convinced they wanted me for breeding purposes. Why would anyone want to propagate life on this horrible planet?

Then I realized that in spite of everything, mankind's instinct for survival reigned supreme. Perhaps they felt that producing offspring would help to create a new and better world than the one they had left behind. They would teach the young about the mistakes made on earth, educate them in what they knew of medicine, engineering and space exploration. In essence, with new life they could construct a Utopia. And the irony was that it was exactly why my team had been sent here.

It became my obsession to know everything about

the Cosmonauts' intentions, not only their initial purpose when they set out on their mission before landing on this planet, but their intentions towards me and my crew. Sequestering myself from Reynard and his prying eyes, I studied the book, memorizing the patterns of the Cyrillic letters, the repetitions, and comparing them to common and repeated words in English. Soon I was able to decipher sentences, though pronunciation of what I read was difficult. Late that afternoon, when one of them brought me a meal, I decided to try my new knowledge.

"Spasiba," I said, nodding and smiling.

The Cosmonaut dropped the food in surprise and a cacophony of babbling and chortling brought the other two scrambling over as fast as their stunted limbs could take them. Reynard stood frowning near the hut, watching the entire episode.

The one who had brought my food pointed at me, babbling his incoherent language. He spoke so fast I did not recognize any of the words I'd been trying to learn.

"Puzhalsta." I smiled again, motioning with my hands, palm down, to speak slower. They began crying and carrying on in such a way that it was pointless to attempt anything more for the moment. Reynard sauntered over to me and they moved away, still cackling in wonderment. He appeared to be making an effort to look friendly, but inside I knew he was seething. I had made a breakthrough and he hadn't. That angered and concerned him.

"What did you say to them?" he demanded.

I smiled ever so sweetly. "I just said 'please' and 'thank you'." Which was entirely the truth. "You should try it sometime."

His eyes deepened into that storm cloud black that could terrify others, but not me. "Teach me what you know."

I just laughed. "Fuck off," I said, picking up the book and walking away.

He jumped toward me and grabbed my arm. Suddenly his feet shot out from under him. He landed flat on his face in the rocks, his wail of pain reverberating across the cavern. One of the Cosmonauts had witnessed the altercation and come to my rescue. My heart soared. Another Cosmonaut moved forward and together they clumsily looped a woven rope made of sinew around Reynard and dragged him toward the hut. There they bound him with his back against a stone.

I walked over to my rescuers, gave them a smile that could light up the universe, made a slight bow, and said, "Spasiba!"

From then on it seemed I could do no wrong in the opinion of the Cosmonauts. With each contact I made a supreme effort to use a new English word, and they taught me the Russian words for the food, water, rocks, and anything else we could think of that surrounded us. To speed things up and help me with pronunciation, I would point to a picture in their book, then they would say the word, and I would repeat it until they grinned one of their ghastly smiles and exclaimed, "Da!" Or if I mispronounced the words, which happened often, they would roar with laughter and say, "Nyet!"

I took it upon myself to try and learn their names. The elderly man was Aleksei Ledovsky. The one who had initially brought me to the encampment, Andrei Mitkov, and then there was the third whose name I tried to remember, but was more difficult. Serenti Shiborin; that was it. Identifying or telling them apart in any way other than size and shape was nearly impossible because they all looked alike with their bluish skin and blackened, if not completely missing digits.

Reynard caught me gazing at their hands one day and remarked, "Hydrogen narcosis. Like getting too much hydrogen and not enough oxygen when you're deep sea diving. With prolonged exposure, which they must have had after landing, there is a loss of circulation. Then necrosis and gangrene sets in..." He shrugged. "Well, you see what has become of them. Why they're not mad as hatters as well, I couldn't tell you."

One thing had been puzzling me all along, and I hadn't reached the level of Russian to where I'd been able to ask the Cosmonauts. "Do you think they created this," I waved my arms to encompass the terrarium to which we'd been brought, "or did they discover it?"

"You'll have to ask them once your Russian gets better," Reynard replied, sarcasm heavy in his voice. "I have no idea."

Even more disturbing was what I was learning from the contents of their book. Though Reynard was the enemy and I was not allowed to go too near him as they seemed to fear he would harm me, I knew he'd understand more of the schematics in the book than I did. My best hope would be to keep learning the language and improve my communication then ask what their mission had been about. I was beginning to suspect that their mission had much more dire consequences than just space exploration.

But with each new stride of progress I made, Reynard became more and more disgruntled. He tried copying what he'd heard me say, trying out his Russian pleases and thank you's, but they just spat at him. He'd shrink away once they began their cackling laughter. If the circumstances had been different, if I'd been in a foreign country on a holiday and enjoying myself with newfound friends, it would have been wonderful. Instead, learning the language was no more than a means to an end, to try and complete the mission and get back to earth safely. How the Cosmonauts would feel about me leaving and returning to earth I tried not to imagine. I had become their pet, their child, and with rising dismay, I knew leaving them would be difficult, if not impossible. The question was, when the time for me to depart came, would they let me go?

XII

T-15

With only a week left to harvest specimens and another week needed for travel, it was getting perilously close to the projected date for our team to return to earth. Whether the remaining three had been able to keep gathering samples with only half the crew, or had ceased to discover anything new and reached the quota we'd been sent out here for, I had no way of knowing. It was possible none of them were even still alive. They could have met a similar fate as Sig. There were a million questions I needed to ask the Cosmonauts, not the least of which was why they hadn't returned to our ship to capture the rest of the team.

As my Russian improved, so did their English. I learned that they had been taught some English before their voyage, but had reverted back to their mother tongue once they'd landed. Like anything learned once though, it comes back with practice. Communication between us became easier. And with communication came a trust. I needed to know from them what had happened to Sigma.

"When we first found your ship we did not know your intentions," Aleksei said, in a mixture of Russian and English. "The insignia on your ship was unfamiliar. It looked neither American nor Russian, though we thought it was from earth. We had no need to attack; for our safety we wanted to get one of you alone to question why you were here."

"Why did you murder Sig?" I asked, anger simmering just below the surface. I hadn't forgotten the shrine in the enclosure outside this ecosphere in which I now lived. The gruesome display would be etched into my brain for the rest of my life. "Why was it necessary to kill him?"

The Cosmonaut stared at me through his nearly blind eyes. "We did not kill him. We tried to save him. We have a very bad enemy on this planet. It is zmey," he struggled for the word then shook his head, apparently at a loss to explain. "No, not zmey. It is Aždaha. Only Aždaha."

I hadn't a clue what he was talking about. He searched the ground around us then picked up a sharp-edged rock in his stumpy hand. Though it obviously caused him great pain, he scraped a large crude drawing in the gravel at our feet. As it took form I saw a long body, a serpentine tail, three heads, pointed teeth. Three rows of them, in fact. Like a shark. I studied Aleksei's hideous face and saw a deep-seated fear beneath the deformities. Then I glanced down and saw what he'd drawn.

"A dragon?" I asked, incredulous.

He nodded vehemently. "Da!" He shook his head and said in a grave tone, "Zlo. Zlo." And I knew from what I'd been learning that this meant evil. Very, very evil.

"The..." I paused, trying my best with the pronunciation, "the Aždaha attacked Sig?"

"Da."

"How did you get Sig's hands and feet away from it?"

He made a tugging motion. I almost got sick. He looked at me with such sadness I suddenly had a revelation. Though they hadn't been able to rescue Sig, they'd managed to save Sig's hands and feet. And because they'd lost their own, they'd created a shrine to him, and to the hands and feet they had lost to this beautiful, evil Planet Hell.

"Where did the Aždaha come from?"

Aleksei shrugged. "I do not know. After the crash landing on this planet we soon ran out of food. We hunted and found the lizard. We called it Aždaha because it looked like the dragons in our legends. And we knew that it too must eat so we had hope for our survival."

I finally felt confident enough in our communication and trust to ask the enormous question that had been burning in my brain since we'd been brought to their ecosystem.

"How did you come to be on this planet?"

A flash of pride crossed Aleksei's gruesome visage, allowing a modicum of human expression to break through.

"We were sent in an early test of the R-5A rocket conversion to explore Mars. Our instrument controls began to malfunction. Before we were able to communicate with the Chief Designer, the oxygen levels dropped and we lost consciousness. The rocket crashed on this planet, but we had no way of knowing where we were.

"Though we were not able to restore the ship in any way, we examined the engine and mechanical system and found that they had been sabotaged. But who would want to sabotage our mission? Certainly not Russia. We had no reason to suspect any other country and finally reached the conclusion that, because the United States was desperate to beat the USSR into space, it was the CIA who sabotaged our controls.

"Then you'll be pleased to learn that the CIA no longer exists," I said. "They, like the FBI and all the other so-called "intelligence" agencies of the world, were obliterated during the last war. Just as all the nuclear weapons and plans for building them were ordered destroyed. From what the elders say, it was a good thing."

"KGB?" asked Aleksei.

"They're not around anymore either," I said with a laugh. "There are no borders, boundaries, or autonomous countries. English is the only language allowed. Now it's a new world order, the Order of World Leaders. Of course there have been plots to overthrow them, but because that is high treason, once the traitor is discovered it's an immediate death sentence for them."

Aleksei's face grew troubled and we fell into an awkward silence as he contemplated the demise of his homeland. Trying to lift his mood, I patted his arm, averting my gaze from his decayed hands.

"It's not so terrible; it's probably much like the Russia you once knew. Most people in the city live in communes and those on the outskirts live on collective farms, although the farms are dying from lack of phosphorous to fertilize the soil. We came to this planet in search of a place to relocate earth's people."

When Aleksei didn't reply, I glanced at him. Although he kept his expression guarded from me, I could tell my words had angered him.

"What is earth's population now?" he asked, his voice artificially light.

"No more than a hundred thousand," I replied. "The OWL is contemplating limiting the birth rate to one child per couple."

"You see how we live," he said, "this planet would not be able to support that many people, even if they did not have children. Soon this planet would be as dead as earth."

Suddenly I realized that our conversation had taken a curve down a dangerous road. I had to reassure him that, even if our people were to relocate, he and the other Cosmonauts would not be in danger of losing their home to us, even if I didn't fully believe it myself.

"It seems that without the rest of my team's knowledge, Reynard has been commissioned to bring back phosphorous to rehabilitate earth. This was not part of our mission, but if it will save the planet, it will be a good thing," I said. "Much better than trying to move an entire race of people to another solar system."

I stood, indicating that there would be no point in continuing the conversation. If Aleksei and the Cosmonauts considered us a threat to their lives here, we could all be in danger.

He motioned toward Reynard, sitting outside the hut: a simmering seething being, no doubt plotting his escape and revenge.

"Zlo," he said, and inclined his head at Reynard.

"Da," I replied. "Zlo."

In spite of my increasing success in communicating with the Cosmonauts, I was not naive in believing everything they told me. Deep down I felt that if I were to ask them increasingly detailed information about their mission, I might not get complete accuracy in their answers. My earlier questions had been met with an evasiveness that at first I thought was due to a lack of understanding. Then I came to realize that they deliberately held back details. And why shouldn't they, I asked myself. They knew almost nothing about us because I'd been just as evasive about our mission.

The more I came to understand of what I read in their book, the more concerned I became. While history textbooks and lore might have given their reason for space exploration to be that of curiosity toward other galaxies, alien life forms, or even potential colonization of other planets, the diagrams told a different tale. The word Sloika, appeared in several instances, along with the names Andrei Sakharov and Viktor Davidenko. And it wasn't very long before I came to the conclusion that my sweet, disfigured Cosmonauts had been on a secret mission. A mission to procure, unseen by the rest of the world, massive amounts of hydrogen for the former Soviet Union to produce nuclear weapons.

XIII

My newly discovered knowledge filled me with such dread that I found it difficult to sit with the Cosmonauts and converse with them as I had. It was the same dismaying shock at discovering that your best friend is a closet pedophile or the gentle old man down the street is really a Nazi war criminal. I felt betrayal and disenchantment and couldn't quite understand why. It wasn't as if they'd portrayed themselves as anything other than what they were, which was Soviet astronauts on a space mission. No different from what we were doing, except our mission was for peaceful reasons, to preserve human life by colonizing another planet.

I wondered if Reynard suspected what I already knew. Since the Cosmonauts had kept him in bondage, he hadn't been privy to our conversations or, since I'd had custody of it, access to the book. And yet, I knew he was one smart, canny son-of-a-bitch. Though it had taken me a while to figure things out and I had the book in which to assist me, if he were given just a tiny amount of the information I'd learned it wouldn't take him nearly so long. It was imperative to stay ahead of him.

My problem now was that I needed to regroup with my team. And I had to do that as innocuously as I possibly could so as not to antagonize the Cosmonauts. So far they had only treated me with reverence and respect. But it would not be possible for me to leave or even escape without their assistance. If this Aždaha dragon existed as they said it did, and if Sig's death were any indication, I didn't stand a rat's chance in hell of getting back to the ship alive.

Because it was the Cosmonauts, not the Aždaha, who had taken Reynard and me, they still had the gear I'd carried in my utility belt. This consisted of my communicator, a light stick, and some basic weapons and mining gear. They weren't survival tools by any means, but if I got them back it would increase my chances of making it back to the ship. If I asked the Cosmonauts to let me go and they refused, they'd know I'd try to escape sooner or later. But no doubt an escape attempt would already be assumed, for why would I not want to be back with my own people and return to earth as we planned? Just as that was probably what they'd wanted all this time.

Then it occurred to me that perhaps the Aždaha story was a ruse, a nightmare tale to tell the children to keep them in check. Had the Cosmonauts just told me that story to keep me from attempting an escape? Could I risk not believing it? Now that our communication lines were less blurred I decided to try another tactic: appeal to their humanity. Explain what our mission here was about.

I'd become closest to Aleksei and often helped him with gardening the edible vegetation they grew in hydroponic conditions, as little real soil existed on this rocky planet. Because their hands were so useless even for the most rudimentary of tasks, I took it upon myself to prepare meals from the plants. I allowed Reynard a moment of freedom, recruiting him to prepare the lizard meat, which they either dried or ate raw.

Never having eaten meat of any kind, I had no desire to start, though it appeared our survival might be dependent on lowering my standards. With the high presence of white phosphorus on the planet, no cooking could be done or open flames used. Biting back my revulsion, I utilized my culinary skills and delighted them by rolling up raw lizard strips with vegetation, sushi style.

After serving Andrei and Serenti, and dropping Reynard's food at his feet, I sat alongside Aleksei for a heart-to-heart conversation.

"Aleksei, you and the others have treated us very well. But we are not your guests, we are your prisoners." I waited for a response but he just kept his head down, concentrating on working the food into his mouth and past his rotted teeth.

"We were sent from earth on a mission to harvest specimens from this planet. earth will eventually shrivel and die so we need a new planet to inhabit soon. Our people do not have enough food and water to survive. There is no phosphorous to fertilize the crops, and barely enough water for human consumption and watering crops. Animals are no longer raised for meat, and pets are only allowed on a limited basis and by special permission. Unless we are allowed to complete our mission and return, all our people will die. They are your people, too, Aleksei." He looked up at that and his expression was sad and full of regret.

"Zeta, you are beautiful and fair, like Slavic women."

I smiled, realizing we hadn't yet discussed the OWL or life on earth as it possibly now either existed or did not. In his mind it was as he remembered, with powerful countries vying against each other in trade, commerce, and technology. Threats or concessions fueled by age-old feuds.

"You do not leave," he said. "You stay and make life on this planet." He waved his arm around the compound. "You and Reynard make malyshka." He made a cradling motion with his arms, and rocked. Then he cackled, exposing a foul, toothless grin.

I shuddered and choked back my impulse to gag at the thought of having a baby with Reynard. I shook my head. "No malyshka with Reynard," I said firmly and rolled my eyes. "Definitely, no malyshka.

"But Aleksei," I implored, "my crew needs me. They do not have enough time to complete the mission without Reynard and me. We need to leave."

He stood, the food that had been balancing on his lap falling to the rocky surface at his feet.

"No," he mumbled, "you stay here. You and Reynard make malyshka. Grow food." He stopped and I saw his eyes well up with tears, threatening to overflow. "Stay with Aleksei and Cosmonauts."

And then I realized that their mission had changed. They had been here for more than a hundred rotations with nothing to live for except sheer persistence to survive. They were dying in increments. We were their only salvation, or hope for a future. They might as well be dead if we left. And why they hadn't just walked out and let themselves be eaten by an Aždaha, assuming those mythical creatures were real, I couldn't say.

XIV

T-10

As much as I felt empathy toward the Cosmonauts, my yearning to get back to what was left of my team, complete the mission and return to earth was much stronger. I felt lost being unable to communicate with Lucian, whom I hadn't spoken to since we'd left earth. It was apparent that the Cosmonauts were not going to release us; therefore we needed to come up with a scheme for our escape. It would require Reynard's help, of course. We had only a few days left. He and I would formulate a plan, I would free him and together, with any luck, we could make it back to the ship in time before the rest of the team left.

During meal times Reynard's wrist bindings were removed so he could eat, though his feet remained shackled. As I was the most mobile of anyone in the encampment, it was usually me who served the food. Reynard was occasionally used for labor, but only under strict supervision. I set the evening meal before him, then went around back and untied his wrists.

"We have to plot an escape," I whispered as I unfastened the bindings. "I've talked to Aleksei and there's no way they're going to let us go. After you've finished your food I'll come back and retie you, but I'll make it loose enough that you'll be able to get free. When they're sleeping we'll make a break for it."

"We'll need weapons, supplies, anything we can grab and carry," Reynard hissed back. "If we meet up with this dragon they talked about, we won't have anything to fight it off with. After seeing what happened to Sig, throwing rocks wouldn't be enough. I say we kill the Cosmonauts and take whatever weapons are here."

I fell back and moved so I could face him. "Kill them?" I glanced around quickly to make sure we weren't overheard. "They've managed to survive for decades under the worst conditions and circumstances imaginable. Even though they captured us, they've been kind. How could we, in all good conscience, murder them now?"

"Simple, Zeta. It's them or us. From the beginning of time, the question between warring people and nations has always been them or us. Besides, they're dying. And they're not dying in a good way. They're dying a horrible, lingering death. Honorable men, which they appear to be, would want a quicker death than what they've been suffering. I say we'd be doing them a favor."

I stared at him, numb with the truthful weight of his words. He was absolutely right, but I couldn't do it. I could escape, but I couldn't kill them.

Setting my jaw firmly I said, "I will not kill them except in self-defense should they come after us. We will leave tonight when they're all asleep. In the meantime, I'll make a pretense of tidying up while I'm looking for my gear and any weapons they might have. When I think we're in the clear, I'll come for you."

He nodded, but I could see in his eyes that he wouldn't hesitate to kill if his life were threatened. Whether by the Cosmonauts, my team, or me.

When the Cosmonauts had their bellies full of lizard sushi, I brought around a tea of sorts that I'd made from dried leaves left to soak in water. I knew that the leaves had medicinal properties that relaxed the body and helped initiate sleep. I made a big production about having a cup myself, though in fact, what was in my cup was just water. While I waited for the relaxants in the tea to take effect, I went about tidying the hut and in turn, searched for where my tools were kept.

Soon the three Cosmonauts were snoring their rancid, vibrating snores and I was able to move more freely. If I were discovered I could simply curl up where I was, feigning sleep. They trusted me and had left me unfettered almost since the first day of captivity, perhaps feeling that because I was a woman, and in their culture most women had not yet held high positions of rank or authority, that I was harmless. They were wrong.

Eventually I discovered what I was looking for in the same place that they kept their prized book, radio and nesting doll. From our conversations I now knew that the Russian nesting doll had been given to Andrei by his mother when he was a child. I yearned to be able to take the book, but it was large and cumbersome, and the pages were fragile. I would need to commit its contents to my memory. Besides, it wasn't mine, it was theirs. I wasn't going to steal personal possessions from them.

My pistol, light and communicator were underneath the book. I found my knife had been used as a bookmark between the pages, so I grabbed that and placed it in my utility belt. Some dried roots that contained a high percentage of glucose they were fond of were drying in an earthenware bowl, so I snatched a couple of those. Then I made my way out of the hut, checked on the snoring Cosmonauts, and found Reynard.

"It's time," I growled, "are your arms free?" He nodded. I reached down and helped him untie his feet. He tried to stand and winced, nearly giving us away with his loud groan. I glared at him in the dim, unchanging light.

"I'm okay," he said. "Do you remember the way?" I nodded, pointing in the direction of the tunnel we'd come through what now seemed like many rotations earlier.

"Then let's go," he said, and began to lead the way.

I turned and took one last look at the ecosphere that had been my home for the past few weeks. Lying prone, deep in their own dreams, our incredibly kind, pathetic Cosmonauts slept on, oblivious to our imminent departure. I gave a silent prayer that our stay with them had given them a renewed purpose in life, and maybe a short glimpse of happiness, and that our leaving would not throw them into a final despair from which they could no longer live through.

XV

"Stop!" Reynard's terse whisper brought me up short and I almost rammed into him. We'd just entered the tunnel to make our escape into the outer enclosure.

"What's the matter?"

"I need to go back for a minute. I forgot something."

I grabbed his arm. "No. If you return it's possible that you'll wake them. Didn't you get your tools you had at the harvest site? You weren't carrying any weapons when they captured us." As our prisoner, even if he were in danger outside the ship, we couldn't take the chance of having him armed.

He shook his head. "Wait here. If I'm not back in five minutes start moving down the tunnel. I'll catch up."

I gave him a stony look.

He shrugged. "If I don't come back, go on without me."

Reluctantly, I finally nodded. I didn't have much choice. Although my pistol was safely stashed in my utility belt, I'd have to do more than threaten him with it to stop him. And of course, if I fired it, well that would give away our escape. But of course, he knew all that.

So, I sat just inside the tunnel and waited for what seemed like an eternity. Finally I saw him creeping rapidly toward me, a large bundle under his arm.

"What was it you needed so bad?" I asked.

He opened the bundle to reveal the Cosmonauts' book. My mouth fell open.

"You son-of-a-bitch! They'll never let that pass. They will come after us now."

He rewrapped the book. "They don't scare me. Their only weapon is stealth and now I know how weak they really are they're no threat to us. Keep moving." With that he squeezed out in front of me in the tunnel, the book clutched tightly underneath one arm.

What did he want it for? I wondered. It was old and antiquated. In the past it would have had a place in a library or archives. But any reference to nuclear weapons, or instructions on how to construct them, had been, along with the weapons themselves, destroyed. The data in the book would be banned from public scrutiny, just as speaking or writing in foreign languages was forbidden. It was against the OWL doctrine. Simply being in possession of something like that, with detailed instructions on how to make a hydrogen bomb, would get him court-martialed at best. A death sentence at worst. I smiled to myself at that point because I really didn't care what happened to him, one way or the other.

We retraced the steps that unknowingly we'd taken several weeks before, finally ending up in the gigantic enclosure that seemed almost like a Roman amphitheater where a slave would be set to fight lions. I wanted to find the cave where I'd seen the shrine to Sig, bring back the letter from his helmet and give it to Xi. I wouldn't bring her anything else, though. Knowing what we were up against with the Cosmonauts, I didn't have the same fear of the unknown. I was quite certain they wouldn't hurt me, even if we had the book. I couldn't have said the same for Reynard.

Circumventing the giant enclosure, we eventually found the tiny cave with Sig's remains. I plucked the Σ from the pile and tucked it into my utility belt. Forcing back the nausea I grasped Sig's hand and attempted to pry the ring off the finger. The finger broke away with a snap, dropping the ring to the ground. I picked it up and placed it in my belt to give to Xi. Then we made our way around the periphery, searching for an exit.

"Why the hell did those bastards build it like this," Reynard grumbled, "there's no sign of any tunnel to the exterior, nothing. They couldn't have just teleported in and out of here. Not to mention, they were dragging our asses as well."

He stopped and gazed all around the enclosure. Impenetrable twelve-foot walls as far as the eye could see, just rock, layered upon rock, layered upon more rock. I wondered if the Cosmonauts had actually constructed it themselves, or if an earlier life form were responsible. Or perhaps it was just a natural formation that had always been present. Leaving the ecosphere was not a subject we'd covered in our conversations.

At that moment I noticed a prominent series of ridges in the rocks that would have been evident if there had been light and shadows.

"Look over there," I said, "can you tell what that is?"

He responded by setting off in the direction of the rocks.

We crossed the compound and reached the ridges, which turned out to be rows of steps carefully recessed into the wall. Virtually undetectable, they were sturdy enough to carry even the heaviest of men, including those dragging bodies as the Cosmonauts had with us, and yet articulated in such a way as to cryptically twist and double back. A series of puzzle-stairs to confuse an enemy. I glanced at Reynard.

"This is it," he said, and started climbing. When he reached the top he stood, gazing far off into the horizon. I clambered up behind him. As far as the eye could see there was only a dim purplish haze, no shadows, no light, just a few darker shapes that were probably varying elevations of jagged rocks, smothered in the frightening sameness of a violet neon void.

"Do you have any idea in which direction the ship might be?" I asked. "They brought us here unconscious. There's no way to tell what time of day it is or what direction we're facing. There's no sun, the constellations are like nothing I've ever seen..." I stopped because my voice had become shrill from panic. He turned to me.

"Let's get down the wall first," he said. "You still have your communicator, right?"

I nodded.

"Okay, let's see if we can get hold of the crew and maybe they can guide us toward the ship." He scrutinized me and for the first time I saw actual doubt on his face. "To be honest with you, I haven't a bloody clue where the base is from here."

When we reached the bottom of the exterior wall we stopped and leaned against it while I tried the communicator. I got a couple of screeching squeals, but not much else. I glanced up at Reynard.

"Too far away?"

He frowned. "Maybe." He appeared lost in thought for a moment. "I'm reluctant to start out in any one direction in case it's the wrong one. We'd have to backtrack, and how would we know if it's wrong? Or we'll just wander around in circles until we die. We have only enough supplies to keep us alive for no more than a day or two."

I thought of the foods I'd been able to squirrel away in my belt, and realized that he was right, there wasn't much. Not to mention, we had only a couple of days until the scheduled return launch. By now the team would have given up on our survival, done what they could to harvest the rest of the samples, and be readying the ship for the return flight. If they were still alive.

I scrambled back up to the top of the wall and scanned the horizon. It was only a guess, maybe more than that, a hunch, but there appeared to be a route that appeared less formidable, less rocky. I pointed it out to Reynard.

"That way," I said. "I've got a feeling the ship is in that direction."

He raised his eyebrows, but as he had no more inclination than I which way to go, it was worth a try.

By my reckoning we'd walked for several hours without any sign of the ship or the harvest site set-up. We'd tried the communicator a few times without any results. Finally, Reynard said, "Let's take a break and think about this for a few minutes."

We found a series of flatter rocks to sit upon and rested our feet. Our gear was not made for hiking rocky terrain and had deteriorated with all the walking we'd done. I worried that the soles would wear out and if that happened, our feet, and our bodies, would be exposed to the cold air and rocks. We wouldn't last long once that happened.

I opened my utility belt and took out some of the sugary roots and gave Reynard one to chew on for an energy replacement, then stuck one in my mouth through the helmet opening. For a few minutes I didn't loathe him; we were in the same situation, not of our own making, and for once we were on the same side. I heard a skittering sound then and glanced down. A tiny lizard ran over my boot. I sucked in a ragged gasp; it had three heads.

"Jesus H. Christ!" I squealed. Reynard laughed.

"It's just a mutant lizard," he said, "calm down." He held it in his hands while the thing twisted and squirmed to get free. Without warning, one of the thing's heads bit his finger, though it couldn't do any damage through the heavy Kevlar glove. He almost dropped it, but squeezed it hard instead, giving it a shake.

"Little fucker!" he said.

I laughed. "Hey, it's only trying to get free, just like we are."

He grinned, but didn't let go of the lizard.

I made a face. "Let's get moving. What are you going to do with it?"

He held it up close to his helmet visor and said, "Hello, dinner." He turned to me. "I think we need to hang on to it. It might be the only protein we get."

My stomach flip-flopped. I turned away as he grabbed a rock and got ready to whack it over the head. Then just as I turned, I heard a roar of anger and found myself face to face with the lizard's mother. A furious, fifteen foot tall reptile that left no doubt it was what the Cosmonauts referred to as the Aždaha. A three-headed dragon as legend would have us believe, and a very pissed-off mama lizard. A monitor lizard on steroids. And there was more than one baby. A lot more.

"Drop it!" I shouted, and when he hesitated, I screamed, "No, throw the fucker. Now!"

For once Reynard did as he was told. He tossed the baby lizard in the mother's direction and together we sprinted as fast as our legs would carry us across the rocky landscape. I could hear her scrambling behind us as she first confirmed her offspring was intact then made the decision to pursue or stay with it. Pursuit won out.

We ran until our legs protested in pain. And then Reynard tripped. Down he went, with the lizard right after him. Straddling him, she slashed at the vulnerable spot beneath his helmet. I grabbed a handful of sharp rocks and started pelting her. She turned and opened her mouth to reveal three rows of flesh-ripping teeth.

I reached into my utility belt and pulled out my pistol. I couldn't remember the last time I'd used it and hadn't even checked to see if it still held charges. I cocked the thing, aimed and fired right between her eyes. The blast bounced off her like I'd hit her with a spitball.

"Fuck!" I cocked it again, aimed directly into one of her soulless black eyes and fired.

With a bellow of agony she flipped over backwards, righted herself and came at me. I got ready to fire again, this time at the other eye, and missed. Her tail, an appendage resembling an enormous boa constrictor, whipped around and caught my shoulders. I tumbled over the rocks and landed on my back, the pistol flying from my hands. Out of the corner of my eye I saw Reynard leap for it. He took aim as the lizard reached down to claw at my face. His shot hit its other eye. With an ear-splitting roar she keeled over, kicking violently in the gravel until she died.

"Watch out!" Reynard shouted. The ground appeared to be moving around us. Hundreds of miniature versions of the dead lizard surged forward, covering its body. They ripped at its flesh, gobbling and choking as they greedily swallowed the meat.

I jumped back and ran to get clear of them. But they appeared to take no notice of me in their feeding frenzy. I shuddered then glanced at Reynard.

"That's cold," he remarked, nodding toward the rapidly disappearing carcass of the mother.

"No shit," I replied, taking slow breaths to try and calm my heart rate. I hesitated for a second. "Thanks for that. You probably saved my life. If she hadn't devoured me, her little demons most certainly would have."

He laughed. I couldn't help but follow suit—a necessary form of release. Nothing like a near-death situation to make comrades out of enemies.

"Now I know why the Cosmonauts created the exit stairs with all the switchbacks. That bitch wouldn't be able to climb after them with that battering ram tail of hers. Doesn't seem to stop the babies, though, as they seem to be a major food…"

Reynard stopped me mid-sentence and held up his hand.

"Listen!" he said. "Did you hear that?" I shook my head.

"What was it? More lizards?"

"I thought I heard a shot, right after I fired." He opened the pistol and checked to see how many charges were left. Two remained. He flipped it closed.

"What are you going to do?"

"I think that was the team firing a response to our shot, to let us know where they are. Or for us to tell them where we are. I'm going to fire one shot off and then we listen."

"Not such a good idea," I said, "if we run into another one of those things we'll need everything we've got."

"I don't think we will. If there are more of them the smell of fresh meat will attract them far more than our scent." He stared at me. "Ready?"

I nodded, plugging my ears with my gloved fingers. He raised the pistol and fired a single shot into the air. Then we waited. Within a few seconds we heard a corresponding shot, well off course of the direction we'd been traveling. I glanced at Reynard.

"You don't think it could be someone else?"

He shrugged. "If they've got a gun and are firing in response to us, they're probably human. At this point I'm quite happy to take my chances with any humans we find. Cosmonauts excepted." He headed in the direction the shot had come from then turned back when he realized I hadn't followed.

"Zeta, we need to get moving."

Instead I held out my hand. "My gun, please." He gave me a rueful smile and handed it over, butt first. I tucked it into my utility belt.

"We'd better make tracks. That shot didn't sound so far away that they won't wait for us now."

We set off at a fast clip and when we'd walked for about ten minutes, I tried my communicator again. The line was raspy and hard to hear, but finally a male voice came over the line.

"Zeta?"

"Omega, it's me," I said, so thrilled to hear my team mate I felt tears start up in my eyes. "Reynard's with me. We're heading back to camp. Should be there soon."

"Zeta, there's something…" With a hiss and a crackle the line went dead. Reynard gave me one those unsettling smiles of his, the kind that makes you feel like you've been stripped of your clothes and exposed to the world. Makes you feel vulnerable and nervous.

"Nothing that can't wait for a few more minutes," he said.

I got a sinking feeling in the pit of my stomach at that moment. Under the pretense of being fatigued, I made a concerted effort to keep him just ahead of me and leading, while I stayed two arm's lengths behind. I wouldn't stand a chance if he tried to overtake me and wrestle me for the pistol. Then he'd be in charge and who knew what would happen once we got to the ship.

The rest of our trek went without incident, though, and after what was probably another half-hour of walking we met up with Omega, heading toward us on the Explorer. He threw it into park and leapt forward, grabbing me in a bear hug.

"Where the hell have you been? We'd about given you up for dead." He stepped back and studied me, stared hard at Reynard, noticing that Reynard was not bound in any way, then back to me. He threw me a questioning look then said, "No worries, you can fill me in when we get to the ship."

I climbed in the back seat and made Reynard sit up in front beside Omega so I could keep an eye on him now that we were on opposite sides again. When we reached the encampment, Omega got out and said to Reynard, "Sir, I'm afraid we'll need to put you in restraints again." Reynard sent me a questioning look, but I avoided his eyes. Dutifully he placed his hands behind his back while Omega cuffed him. Then Omega led him off to the security of the ship's staterooms.

Having heard our arrival, the remaining team, Xi, Chi and Rho, came running out to greet me. I fought back tears. After all I'd been through no one would have blamed me, though I'd reached a threshold of maturity that doesn't come from mere training, but through experience. Hard won, at that.

Rho took my hand and led me toward the ship. Her nose wrinkled in distaste. "Once you're cleaned up we need to have a meeting," she said. "There have been a few developments since you've been gone. Was it Reynard?"

I turned her around to face me, unable to keep the amazement off my face. "I don't know what you mean. You think Reynard kidnapped me?" From her expression I knew that's what they believed had happened. The most logical explanation given that they had no knowledge yet of the Cosmonauts, or even the lovely Aždaha.

"The answer to that is no. Reynard didn't kidnap me, he didn't hurt me and he just finished saving my life. But I'm glad Omega put him in custody again because we absolutely cannot trust him."

We entered the airlock of the ship together and I headed to the stateroom. Once I'd finished cleaning up and had a bite to eat, we all met in the ship's bridge.

It appeared Omega had taken complete charge of the mission, which was fine by me. I'd had my fill of decision making. It seemed as if being Captain of the ship came naturally to him. I realized to my chagrin that I was beginning to see him in a different light than I had before.

"Zeta," he began, "we don't know what has taken place with you and Reynard over the past couple of weeks, but there are several serious developments that we need to share with you."

I felt a puzzled frown cross my face. Xi leaned over and squeezed my hand. Rho gave me a weak smile.

Omega flushed with embarrassment before he continued. "Sometimes when a person has been in close contact with a captor or…" My hands flew up, palms facing the team.

"Whoa!" I said. "Are you intimating that I might have formed an alliance with Reynard? Who wasn't my captor, by the way. That's what you're suggesting, right? Stockholm's Syndrome. If you are, let me assure that I am very glad that you have him in custody again. He did save my life, but he'd just as easily take it if I were in his way." I took a deep breath, trying to get over my initial hurt feelings. They had no way of knowing what had transpired during my absence.

"Now," I turned and gazed appreciatively at each of them, glad to back in their midst, no matter what they thought of my inadvertent departure with Reynard, "tell me what's happened since I left and after that I'll fill you in on what I've been doing."

XVI

"When we discovered you and Reynard missing," Omega began, "we sent Rho and Chi out to search for you. Naturally we assumed that he had somehow overtaken you and had you as his prisoner. We've been waiting for contact from either one of you, whether he was holding you for ransom, or whatever else he has stored in his evil mind. It was too similar to the situation that happened with him and Sig to assume anything else." He stole a look at Xi, who glanced down at her hands.

"After a couple of days had passed, though, we had to take stock of our options. We were down two more hands in harvesting specimens from the planet. Should we spend our resources looking for you both or concentrate on completing the mission? Without word from either one of you we decided to carry on as best we could. To that end, we needed to communicate with CUB, and with Reynard missing, we had to get the transmitter operational."

He paused, and Xi picked up the thread. "Omega worked night and day and finally got the transmitter to send a message. But before that, he was able to see the last communications that had been sent from our ship."

"I know," I interrupted, "Reynard had informed them we'd all been killed."

Xi shook her head. "That was the first message we found. Reynard sent more later when the transmitter was allegedly not working. It was working all along; he just made it inoperable at his convenience. He rigged it so they thought we were dead and we thought we couldn't communicate with them. He'd figured it out pretty well until Omega took over." She shot him a glance then that suddenly made me almost jealous. I shook it off, chiding myself. I had no claim to him; I had made it plain that I wasn't interested. Not to mention, there was a young man named Lucian back on earth who, for now, I could only dream about in the privacy of my chamber.

"The messages that Reynard sent were confidential and were to one of the OWL leaders, Hermes, the leader of the Quadrant III. Reynard told him he'd found phosphorite. Although the language he used was deliberately cryptic, it seems as if he and Hermes have been working together on a secret mission of their own for quite some time. Not one that is sanctioned by the other leaders of the OWL."

"What do you mean?" I asked, incredulous. "The OWL represents all of earth. They are our leaders. They protect us. They have sent us here to gather specimens of the soil, minerals, and gases to determine if this planet simulates earth enough to make it habitable. Without a planet to colonize now that earth is virtually a wasteland, none of us can live. Earth will never be able to return to its once fertile state."

"Maybe that's what three of the leaders want and believe. But Hermes doesn't," Omega stated. "Hermes wants to overthrow the rest of OWL and form one world order, his world. And he recruited Reynard to do it. That's the purpose of finding a new source for phosphorous to use for fertilizing the crops. I believe this was a multi-faceted mission. Find phosphorous, but in addition, harvest specimens to establish the possibility of relocating to a new planet. If the planet turned out not to be habitable, then they will try to resurrect earth."

I moved over to the ship's console, idly flipping through the communication logs without actually seeing them. The rest of the team waited for me to make a move, help them place Reynard's and Hermes' motivations, and all of the puzzle pieces, together. But I had no more answers than they did.

Chi's voice broke the silence, low and ominous in tone.

"In searching through the messages we discovered that Reynard had been in contact with Hermes multiple times. We think that he disabled and enabled the communications system at will. It seems that while Reynard was out with Sig he discovered the remains of a Soviet era spaceship from the 1960's. He believes that on board was a book of instructions, complete with all the ingredients, of how to build a hydrogen bomb. In the 1950's and 1960's, the United States and Russia were in a race to be the first in space travel. Hermes wants the information the Russians had as all previous technological records and information for producing weapons of mass destruction were eradicated when the OWL assumed command."

I sat there, numb and sick, because I realized that right from the beginning we had all been disposable labor. That our entire purpose, being young, strong and smart, was to bring back the ingredients and knowledge to further destroy earth or other planets, and other lives.

I gazed at Omega, feeling more tired than I had after fighting off the Aždaha and all its nasty babies.

"He missed that piece we brought back the day we found Sig's remains, didn't he?"

Omega nodded.

"Do you think he killed Sig because he discovered what Reynard was up to?"

An uncomfortable quiet settled around us as we considered the grim possibility that our assigned leader was responsible for a crew member's death. I glanced around at each of the team and found no one willing to meet my eyes.

"I can't believe he'd kill one of us," Chi said. He rested his chin in one hand, the light in the room shadowing and accentuating the flawless structure of his face. When he and Rho exchanged glances I saw open admiration shining in her eyes. I mentally crossed my fingers, hoping he would reciprocate her feelings one day. But for now, our survival was at stake. Given the recent events, I wondered how much I should share with the rest of the team to let them know how much danger we were in.

"Reynard has the book," I said.

Omega frowned. "How? And where would he have gotten it? He had nothing with him when I brought you both back in the ATV. He wasn't carrying anything. Nor did he leave it in the vehicle."

I thought back, trying to remember when I'd last seen him with the book. Was it before the attack by the Aždaha? Had he dropped it when we were fighting her off? Or had he stashed it somewhere so it wouldn't be found on him, and he'd be able to retrieve it later? Knowing Reynard as I had come to, I believed it to be the latter. I still hadn't debriefed them about the Cosmonauts though, and now it was time.

"It was the lost Cosmonauts who captured Reynard and me. That was part of their space craft Reynard found," I said. "Let me fill you in on just what we've been doing for the past couple of weeks."

After I'd told my story, the team sat around with their mouths hanging open, quite literally speechless. Finally Chi said, "I think we should bring them back with us to earth. After all, on Hermes' orders, Reynard's purpose after discovering their ship was to bring back the information on building the H bomb. With the information they possessed, think of what else they could tell us."

I shook my head. "They wouldn't make the trip. Though they appear to have developed immunity to death from natural causes such as heart disease or cancer, they are dying by degrees. Like a plant whose roots are still viable, but all the leaves are turning black and falling off. They're gangrenous fossils of their former selves."

"We have Reynard as our prisoner," said Xi, "but how are we going to stop Hermes? Even if Reynard doesn't bring back the book, the phosphorous, and specimens from this planet, he and Hermes will eventually find another way to overthrow the other OWL."

"But without the phosphorous there is no life, remember," Chi said. "Earth has three rotations left at best. Barely enough time to raise crops to sustain the current population. If we return empty handed, we die. If we don't return, we die. Our only evidence of Hermes' plot with Reynard is through their communications, easily disputed. Reynard has reported us as dead. He has more credibility, especially with Hermes on his side, than we do. He could say we held him captive, which is true, because we wanted all the rewards for ourselves. He could say we've been plotting with Hermes."

Rho said, "It looks like no matter what we do, we're fucked."

Chi laughed involuntarily, but stopped immediately at the darkness on all our faces.

I turned to Omega. "How close are we to completing harvesting all the samples and specimens we need?"

"We're nearly done. One day or less and we should have it wrapped up. While you've been gone we decided to also mine as much phosphorous as possible. As much as we can carry." He stole a glance at Xi. "We have extra space in Sig's chamber, should we need it. Or if we were to bring someone back."

The idea of bringing back any of the Cosmonauts was pointless. In any case, none of them would leave without the others. The earth they'd left no longer existed. Their homeland, their people and their culture no longer existed. This was their home now, for all its difficulties. On earth they'd be shunned because of their deformities, their culture, and their language. Maybe the atmosphere here was what kept them preserved as perfectly as it had, well past their natural expiration date. No, they could use Sig's chamber for whatever was needed, but it wasn't going to be to bring a Cosmonaut back to earth.

I considered what we should do, something that I was sure the rest of the team had been wondering as well, especially when they were unaware of our whereabouts. The decisions that had to be made: return without two of their team, or stay and breach the instructions of the mission.

"I'd like to read those transmissions Reynard made," I said. "Maybe the answer lies somewhere within them."

Omega turned to the ship's console and pushed a few buttons, bringing the transmission screen to life. "It begins here," he said, pointing to a message. I moved alongside him to read the messages, wondering if he realized how prophetic his words were.

As I read the transmissions between Hermes and Reynard I was struck by how obtuse they were. Our progress with the harvests was to be reported to the Control Unit Base and not to the OWL, so Reynard communicating with Hermes was suspicious in itself. Except that I could tell nothing from the language that indicated any sort of coup or mutinous plan. Omega was right when he'd said they were cryptic, except that they were so cryptic I couldn't see anything suspicious in them whatsoever, and told him so. They read like regular progress reports, day to day findings, anticipated yield and date of return.

I turned to Omega. "What was in here that you found questionable?" He leaned in to read over my shoulder, frowned, rolled the mouse to advance the messages.

"That's weird," he said. "These are not the same messages I saw."

Xi jumped up and advanced to look in. "That's impossible. We all saw the communications between the two. Hermes referred to The Book, made it sound like the Bible, but it was the way the message was written. They'd capitalize words like 'Hope,' which we took to mean H, or hydrogen. The word 'Prolong' was capitalized, but written in such a way that we figured out it was phosphorite."

She started reading then whirled around. "They're gone!"

Rho raced over. "What do you mean, gone? Deleted?"

"Somehow. But I don't know who could have done it. For security reasons, messages aren't alterable once they've been sent." She shook her head in wonderment and we all stood staring at one another. Reynard was locked up. Who else could have deleted the messages? We all stared at one another, scrutinizing, weighing all we knew about the other, until each one of us eventually dropped our gaze as skepticism formed. Divide and conquer. We knew the concept well. But who was dividing and who would conquer, only one of us knew.

XVII

They gave me a pass on my work schedule because of my earlier travails. With our discovery of the missing communications no one wanted any one of the others to be alone on the bridge. I took the opportunity to have another look at what was supposed to be incriminating messages. If what the team had said were true, that certain messages had gone missing, then none of my team was guilty. They had to have been removed by someone elsewhere. My bet was that it was Hermes, in a movement of self-preservation. As far as he knew, Reynard was right on task and would be bringing back what he had commissioned him to do. And once he had what he wanted, no doubt Reynard would be as disposable as we were.

As I read them over, though, I was struck by something else that apparently the team had missed. All the transmissions that had come from earth had the dates skewed somehow. From the earliest transmissions, the dates of the return messages were at a time well into the future. The messages submitted from earth started off only a few weeks out of sync then they were off by months. But the last one received was ahead of our time by nearly five rotations.

I tried to take in what that meant. Could it be that something was wrong with the transmission equipment? A malfunction, or yet another trick on Reynard's part? Or, what if, and the thought scared me as none other, what if earth's time was different from that on Arianrhod? Was it possible that in a solar system as far away as this our time moved slower? And if that was the case, and earth was five rotations ahead of us, but only had enough phosphorous to grow life sustaining crops for three rotations, what, if anything, still existed there?

My thoughts flew to Lucian. Since we'd arrived on Arianrhod I'd been unable to contact him in any way. Had he been told I was dead? If earth was five rotations ahead of us, had he moved on to someone else? Or was he even still alive? I ached to be able to send him a transmission, tell him I loved and missed him more than I ever thought possible.

I didn't know who I could trust anymore. Anything could have transpired here while Reynard and I were being held captive. The team had learned about the Cosmonauts, and about the book. Fewer of them returning meant more phosphorous could be transported back. That, and whoever would be the highest bidder on the Cosmonauts' book, well, the potential for absolute power was not only real, it was extremely tempting. But tempting enough to betray your team?

In my gut I felt that Rho could be trusted. We'd grown up together in the same compound in Quadrant II, with different names and from different families, of course, but we were as close as sisters. For the moment I erased any doubts from my mind. When she returned to the ship, I took her aside, showed her the dates on the transmissions and told her my theory. Her amber eyes grew wide.

"But that would mean…"

I nodded. "It could mean that nothing exists on earth any more, assuming the scientists were correct in their estimate of having enough phosphorous for three rotations. We're at nearly five rotations now, according to the dates. Life there as we knew it, might be dead. Maybe that's why we haven't had communications from CUB since a few weeks after we arrived here. Their time passes at a rate exponential to ours, roughly 20 times from what I can tell."

She sat, cradling her head in her hands. "Why didn't we see this? Why couldn't Control have noticed that, while a week had passed on earth, only hours had gone by here?"

I shook my head. "I don't have an answer to that. Why didn't anyone see? Because no one looks at that unless they have a reason to. We were so busy searching for other things it didn't stand out. We left it up to the scientists, CUB, the OWL, to determine everything about Arianrhod. Yes, we traveled into the future to get here, but this future moved slower than earth's."

Rho looked up. "Just bad luck."

I nodded. "Very bad luck."

"Do you think anyone or anything there is alive?"

I shrugged and let out a huge sigh. "I have no idea."

I'd long since kept my innermost thoughts about Lucian shuttered, having no ability to speak with him or tell him how I felt. The strain of holding back my fears from my team that we'd never return to those we cared about weighed heavier upon me with each passing day.

When everyone got back from the field, I told them what

Rho and I had discovered and what it could mean for our return. There was an overwhelming sense of failure that fell over everyone. Hard as we'd tried, we'd failed. And the worst of it was, even if we went back, we couldn't prove the time difference. We'd have to suffer the consequences, our punishment, if life still existed on earth. And could we even be part of it?

"What should we do?" Rho asked. "What can we do?"

"I say we try go back to earth according to plan, see what's left. Maybe a small pocket of people survived, maybe the scientist's predictions were off. Maybe we're wrong about the time difference," Xi said. "At any rate, whatever life is left will need the phosphorous to grow crops. It's our duty to preserve and restore as much life as possible. And if there isn't anyone, then our team will be the new pioneers to start over."

"But," I countered, "what if I'm right? If we get there and there's nothing. Even having the phosphorous we're bringing back is no guarantee we'll be able to grow sufficient food fast enough to sustain ourselves. Our fuel supply is limited, and without food and other supplies it would be impossible to locate another potential settlement in the known universe. We'll have made the trip for nothing."

"What do you suggest then?" said Omega. "You seem to have all the answers." Furious, I whirled to face him.

"I don't have any answers, but I could have done a better job of keeping communications open here than you have." Two bright red spots flared in his cheeks and instantly I regretted my words. Who knows how I would have handled things had our situations been reversed.

I offered an apologetic smile to Omega. "I'm sorry.

That was unfair of me."

He just nodded. We were all under a strain and in-fighting was not going to help. We sat pensively, trying to come up with a plan. It occurred to me that we could consult Reynard, who as a former Marine had the ability to adapt, improvise and overcome, no matter how dire the situation. Or…

"What if we send Reynard back to earth alone?" I said. "He can take all the phosphorite he's harvested and accept whatever consequences or reward awaits him there."

"How will that help us?" Rho asked. "Once he leaves and takes the ship we're left here without any means of transport back. Even if life still exists on earth, you can bet he won't send anyone back for us once he's gone. We'll be stranded."

"If we let him go he'll be free to do whatever he wants; go back to earth or set off for somewhere else. There's no point in him staying. And if he has any humanity in him whatsoever, should he encounter human life, he could have them send a rescue mission for us." No one looked very pleased with my suggestion.

"How will we survive here?" Xi asked. "This planet has nothing on it except hydrogen and phosphorite. We couldn't live for very long. Our suits would wear out then we'd end up dying a slow death like the Cosmonauts."

I'd thought about that. They hadn't yet met the Cosmonauts and when they did, and saw how they'd suffered, their belief in forming a life on this planet, however temporary, would be not only nearly impossible, but undesirable. Still, I had given it a lot of thought over the past few weeks, not just since our recent discovery.

"The Cosmonauts came here approximately thirty Arianrhod rotations ago; over a hundred of ours. It took them a long time to adapt and overcome the elements, and find and develop the ecosphere they inhabit." I looked around at each of them, hoping my conviction in the newly forming idea would sink in. "But they adapted even with the limited knowledge of this planet and resources they had to them back then. We can learn from them and continue what they've accomplished.

"If there is one ecosystem they discovered, there may be more. There are not that many of us, what they have could sustain us all for a long time. Maybe long enough for a rescue party, but if not, maybe a life on this planet wouldn't be so terrible."

"Are you really suggesting we stay here to inhabit this place?" Chi asked.

"Yes, I am. Reynard has no need for the Explorer ATV. We could keep that. It runs on hydrogen. As do our weapons. There's no shortage of hydrogen here. We have the Doomsday Kit with basic medicines, and several rotations supply of seeds for everything we'd need to grow to survive. A couple of crops, along with whatever we can get from with the ecosystems on this planet, and we could live a very good life."

I had one more tactic, unfair though it was. "It's not like we have any family, other than ourselves. We're Control orphans. There's no one waiting for us besides the greedy OWL. Why not think of ourselves? What good will all the riches and rewards on earth do for us if the planet is dead? Or we're all that's left once we get back?" I could see they were not convinced. Xi's downcast scowl told me exactly how she felt, while the others' faces mostly held skepticism and fear. I wasn't going to try and talk them into it. They had to see for themselves what was out there for us.

There was something I had to do, though, to make

things right. I would have to find the Cosmonaut's book and return it to them. More importantly, I didn't want Reynard to be able to retrieve it. Who knew what nefarious purposes he could use it for? If he chose to do so, he could annihilate Arianrhod before he left. I stared into the faces of all that remained of my team.

"We need to find the book and return it to the Cosmonauts. I want you to meet them, to see how they live, and what our lives could be like," I said. "Then you can make your decision, stay here or leave with Reynard. He won't harm you if you do go with him. He'll need you as support, moral, physical or whatever.

"In the meantime," I continued, "let's get busy unloading the Doomsday Kit, the ATVs, and splitting whatever additional medical supplies and clothing remains between whoever leaves and those who decide to stay."

Rho walked over and gave me a hug.

"Who's going to tell Reynard?" she said.

I stood, stretched, and flexed my arms. "Might as well be me," I said. "Given the time we've spent together I've gotten to know him better than anyone else here." I left them talking over the plans, not knowing whether they were with me or against me. It didn't matter, whatever the rest of them decided to do, I was going to stay.

But when I entered the stateroom Reynard was nowhere to be found. The cuffs and tape that had been used to secure him and bind his ankles were piled in a heap near the door. I raced to the airlock, but there was no sign of him there either. I considered how long he might have been free, and if he'd heard any of our discussion. I headed to the storage room and looked in at the weapons rack, all were missing. Then I checked our supplies, as well as the location where we kept the Doomsday Kit. Everything was gone, including Reynard.

I ran back to the team who were still animatedly discussing our options. They glanced up in alarm as I stormed into the room.

"What's wrong?" Rho said.

"He's gone. And he's taken everything with him that we need. Except for the ship, of course," I said caustically.

"And the ATV," Chi added. We all glanced at each other, the same thought apparently crossing our minds. Then we heard the sound of a motor revving.

"We need to stop him!" I shouted. We scrambled to the rear of the ship just in time to see the taillights of the Explorer ATV disappearing into the blue-violet horizon. I grabbed my suit and helmet, struggling to pull them on, but it was too late. I'd knew I'd never be able to catch him.

"Shit!" I yelled, stomping up and down. "Shit! Who the hell tied him up?" Despite all the guilty frowns, no one appeared to remember, or seem inclined to take responsibility.

I sat down to think. Reynard had everything that we needed to stay alive, whether we stayed on this planet or returned to earth. Our only hope at survival was to intercept Reynard. He would be retracing his steps to retrieve the book, then, as the ship was filled with hydrogen and readied for takeoff within the next day, he would abandon us. We still had whatever firearms we were carrying on our person, and there might be a stash somewhere in the ship he hadn't had time to loot.

"We've got to get back to the Cosmonauts. I'm going to retrace the route Reynard and I took so we can try and find their book. If we're not too late already." It was time for me to take charge. When it came to Reynard, few knew him better than me.

"Chi, you and Rho stay with the ship and search for any arms and supplies that might still be left. Fill our packs with whatever transportable food and medical supplies you can find. Let me know when the packs are ready." I turned to Omega and Xi.

"I'm not pointing any fingers. He's a slippery fucker. But someone messed up. We need a team to go to the Cosmonauts and someone has to stay here with the ship. When and if Reynard comes back he's probably going to try and take it. I shouldn't have to remind anyone how dangerous he is." I glanced from one to the other. "Who is it going to be?" For a few minutes I thought I was going to have to choose as no one spoke up.

Finally Xi said, "I'll do it. I'm a good shot and I can go a long time without sleeping. If we all have our communicators with us and if I've got enough weapons here, I should be able to hold him off if he comes back."

I met her eyes. "Are you sure? Maybe Chi…"

She shook her head. "No, I'll do it." And from her expression I could see why it was she'd volunteered. The loss of Sig was still uppermost in her mind and she had never stopped blaming Reynard for his death. I hadn't told her about the shrine, nor would I ever be able to share what a violent end he'd met. I could, however, give her something to hold on to.

"I forgot about this," I said, reaching into my utility belt. "Maybe it'll bring you luck." I handed her the Σ from Sig's helmet. She blinked hard a few times then looked up at me with an incredible aching sadness.

"It wasn't very lucky for Sig, though, was it?" I didn't have anything to say to make her feel any better. Then I recalled that I also had her Academy ring that she had given Sig. It felt as if a boulder were lodged against my lungs. I brought out the ring that I'd taken from Sig's withered finger and pressed it into her palm. She knew what it was even before she opened her hand. For a long time she stared at the ring nestled in her palm, its proximity to the one Sig had given her made it appearing as if they were linked. I knew Xi was probably torn between wanting, and not wanting to know how I'd managed to retrieve it.

"He told me it would never leave him." Her shoulders shook. I put my arm around her and she leaned into me as if absorbing as much comfort as possible. A soundless sob wracked her body.

"We grew up together in neighboring collectives in Quad IV," she said. "Did he ever tell you?"

"No, I didn't know that," I fibbed, giving her the opportunity to talk and share if she wanted.

She nodded, smiling at an unbidden memory. We were prevented from conversing further because Rho and Chi had emerged from the ship. Rho dragged five bulging backpacks and utility kits; Chi shouldered an assortment of pistols. Omega and Xi ran up to help them. I stared at Chi.

"We only need enough weapons and supplies for four," I said.

Alarmed, he shot a look to Omega, who nodded. "Xi has volunteered to stay with the Astraeus in case Reynard returns," Omega said, sounding defensive. "Someone has to do it. As long as we retrace the way that Reynard and Zeta returned, we're more likely to meet him out in the field than here."

A pregnant silence followed, not one of us able to meet anyone else's eyes.

"But he has the Explorer ATV," Rho said finally. "He could be anywhere. He'll be able to travel far faster than we can with the Pup or on foot."

"That's why we have to make things more difficult for him," I replied. "Chi and Omega, you need to remove a key part of the ship's operating system so he can't fire it up and leave. Even if he gets back here before we do, he won't have the parts he needs or be able to fix it in time." I turned to Xi.

"If he does return, you need to immediately communicate that to us. If your life is threatened in any way and you are not able to hold him off, take cover until we can get to you, or take the Pup and head out as far as you feel safe. Stopping him is not worth your life." She nodded, her expression as cold and dark as a newly dug grave.

"Do you need him dead or alive?" she said.

We set off on foot, the backpacks and utility belts weighing us down, but not more than the weapons we carried. We were armed and ready to kill if we needed to. I was thankful that the team had let me rest instead of asking me to help harvest the remaining phosphorous. In all likelihood I wouldn't have been able to make another trek without becoming severely fatigued. As it was, I felt buoyed to not only finally stop Reynard for once and for all, I was eager to see the Cosmonauts again. I hadn't filled the team in on the possibility of encountering another Aždaha, I'd just warned them to be aware of alien life. What an understatement that was.

Omega led the way as he was familiar with the first part of the trip from when he met Reynard and me on the ATV. Unfortunately, no landmarks or unusual outcropping of rocks from before were identifiable. Just the same neon-blue and purple haze.

We walked for several hours and finally stopped to rest at the point where Omega had found us. I brought out a bottle of water and handed it to him. He inserted the straw through the mouthpiece of his helmet, took a long drink and passed it back.

"How long do you think you and Reynard walked before we met up?"

"Half a day, maybe. It's so difficult to pinpoint time here, with no sun or moon to indicate a passage of time." Then I remembered the Aždaha. "We probably shouldn't linger anywhere for very long, even with weapons we're rather vulnerable." I stood, slung my backpack on and adjusted it.

"I'll lead from here. There aren't any shadows, but there are lots of these rock ledges and outcroppings. We need to keep an eye out for the Cosmonauts' book, because I'm certain that's what Reynard is looking for as well. If we encounter him, this is where it'll be."

I set off in the lead, Rho scrambling behind me to catch up. Chi and Omega were back a length, scanning for signs of a place Reynard may have hidden the book. I wished I'd taken note of the last time I'd seen Reynard with it, wished even more that I'd forcibly taken it away from him when I discovered he had it.

"How do you know for sure we're heading the right way?" Rho asked. I gave her a brief glance, but all the while my eyes roved the periphery for signs of another lizard. Or her little ones. If there was one, there would be more. At least two enemies out here waiting for us to slip, Reynard and the Aždaha. A comforting thought.

"Gut feeling, mostly. Reynard and I had no idea we were traveling in the right direction when we left the Cosmonauts. It wasn't until we…" I stopped in my tracks and the men almost piled into me.

"You what?" Rho said.

"Until we fired at the Aždaha." I looked at Omega. "That's why you heard us. We shot a lizard. You heard us and fired a shot in response."

"What kind of lizard are we talking about, Zeta?" Chi asked. As we walked, I filled them in as best I could, leaving out some of the last gruesome details.

"It's imperative to be aware of everything around you at all times," I warned. "Whether in the case of the lizards or Reynard. Both would kill you as soon as look at you. Survival on this planet is not for the weak or faint-hearted."

Despite searching every suspicious rocky cairn or likely hiding place, we found no evidence of where Reynard might have hidden the Cosmonauts' book. Exhausted, hungry and thirsty, we finally reached the great wall of the compound, rising like a fortress in the neon blue glow.

"Wow!" said Rho. "Did they build this? It must have taken them forever."

Chi kicked at a rock. "Not like they had much else to do other than try and stay alive. No wonder their fingers are worn down to bone."

"Reynard told me that was from hydrogen narcosis," I said, made a little defensive by their comments when they knew nothing of the Cosmonauts apart from what I'd told them. "Survival meant not only creating a barricade between them and whatever was trying to kill them, it also meant building a sanctuary where they could grow food."

I hunted for the stone staircase leading up the wall. We circumvented it a quarter of the way before we found it. Then we climbed, our movements slow and cautious on the treacherous terrain. I led the way with Omega directly behind me and Chi and Rho following.

We were half way up the steps when we heard Rho let out a bloodcurdling scream. She was near the bottom of the rock steps and pulling at her helmet as if she were having trouble breathing. We scrambled down to assist her just as she yanked off her helmet, dropping it to the ground below. Then she half-fell, half-scrambled to the bottom.

"Rho! What the hell are you doing? There's not enough oxygen in this atmosphere for you to breathe," I yelled. I grabbed her helmet and tried to force it back on her head, but she fought me. Her lips had turned blue. I took a deep breath and pulled off my own helmet. Then I put my mouth over hers and gave her short puffs of air, the breath of life. She responded for a few seconds, but as soon as she started to come around she fought the helmet again. Then she screamed and clawed at something only she could see.

"Get them off!" she shrieked, "get them off me!" Omega grabbed her arms and held them behind her while I forced the helmet back over her head.

"Rho, you need it to breathe," I pleaded. I twisted around to see Chi standing there, shaken and unsure of what to do.

"Get whatever sedatives you can find in our supplies and bring them here," I said. "She's suffering from hydrogen narcosis and having hallucinations. She'll die if we don't sedate her."

While Omega kept her arms pinned, I spoke reassuringly to her until Chi came forward with a syringe of a sedative preparation. I glanced at him with a question in my eyes.

"I hope it's enough," he said. "I took some of the lighter stuff because if she goes out cold we'll never get her up the side of this rock face."

I nodded, grateful for his foresight. I pushed up the injection flap on the sleeve of her suit and inserted the sedative, holding her close until I felt her taut muscles relax somewhat.

"Slide her to a sitting position," I told Omega. I slipped the flap back down and waited for the effects of the sedative to take hold, hoping that she would just be mellow and not go straight to sleep. We couldn't leave her outside the wall, no matter how quickly we acted. Reynard was possibly nearby. Or even an Aždaha, for all we knew. I felt her pulse. It had slowed to a nearly normal rate.

"Help me," I said to Chi. Together we slung her arms over our shoulders, hoisted her between us, and started climbing up the rock wall.

"This isn't going to work," he panted. "I'll stay down here with her while you and Omega get inside."

I shook my head. "Hell, no! You have no idea what it's like out here this far from the camp. We can't take a chance at losing any more of our team." I saw Rho's eyelashes flicker and her eyes focused on me with recognition this time, and not seeing snakes, or lizards, or whatever hallucinations had terrified her.

"Rho?" I gave her a little shake.

"Mmmmm," she murmured.

"Okay, she's better now," I said. "Let's get moving. We don't have much time."

Though her legs wobbled unsteadily, by moving with cautious steps were able to ascend the twisting steps that led to the rocky ledge above. When we reached the top, I turned to Omega.

"Have a long look around the outside periphery," I said, deliberately keeping my voice low. "You might be able to see Reynard and the Explorer. If not, he could very well be still inside the compound. If he is, we need to be prepared for an ambush."

Omega nodded, remaining at the top of the wall for several moments while the three of us descended, then he followed us until we were all standing near the bottom of the steps. I glanced around the now familiar terrain, with its inscrutable rock face, and suddenly was hit with a realization. I knew where I'd last seen the book. It was in the cave with the shrine to Sig. I turned to the others.

"I think I know where the book is," I said. "And of course, so does Reynard because he left it there. Now all we can hope is that we got here before him, if that's at all possible. Follow me."

Staying close to the rock so as not to be exposed should Reynard appear, I moved slowly around the inside center of the compound. I discovered a cave and bent down to enter it, shining my light into the depths not illuminated by the ever present neon. Although I couldn't see anything other than a recessed hole, only large enough for one person at a time moving in single file, I got down on my knees and started to creep inside.

"Zeta," Omega's voice came from behind me, sounding too far back for my comfort level, "do you know what you're doing?"

"Yes," I whispered back. But this wasn't the same cave that I'd been placed in alongside Sig's remains. It was an entirely different one, but it went deeper and further back, to the point where it resembled the tunnel to the Cosmonauts' ecosphere. I pondered on whether to move forward and explore what it held then realized that we needed to find the book first. This cave could wait. I backed out to where the others stood waiting.

"It's the wrong cave," I said. "Though it's worth checking into if we have time. If Reynard's not in the cave where we were held, it could be that he's somewhere in this one."

XVIII

We continued moving around the compound until we found another recessed cavern. This one appeared familiar to me. I shone my light inside and saw the beam bounce off the same blank darkness, no tangible way to tell them apart. Still, I was quite certain this was the one. It was also larger than the last cave had been. I beckoned to my team and they followed me in, all the while checking behind them to make certain they wouldn't be ambushed.

Then we entered a wider space, more open. This was where I'd awakened after having been brought here by the Cosmonauts. I cast my light around and saw the receding shriveled flesh on the hands and feet that were set beneath the piece of Sig's suit. I heard Rho's sharp intake of breath and a sort of a moan escape from Chi. They knew what it was without me even telling them. I turned.

"None of this gets back to Xi, do you hear me?" No one challenged me on that.

Now I needed to look around for the book. I tried to recall what Reynard had been doing when we had last been here and I had taken the Σ and the ring to bring back for Xi. Because he had stolen the book in haste from the Cosmonauts' hut, he had been carrying it wrapped in the loose woven mats they used. He had stopped and tried to squeeze into his utility belt, but it wouldn't fit. He didn't have a backpack like mine because he'd been my prisoner when we'd been captured. So what could he have put it in?

Suddenly Omega held up his hand. "Wait!" he said. "I hear something coming." We all stood stock still, straining our ears for the tiniest of sounds. Then it came, the gentle murmur of the Explorer somewhere in the distance. Omega turned to me.

"Is that the only entrance to the compound that you know about?" I nodded, intuition telling me what was going through his mind.

"It's the only one I'm aware of," I said. "But it's entirely possible there could be more. If we waited near the base of the steps for him to descend we could take him into custody and get on with the rest of the mission, whatever we decide to do."

"Zeta's right," Rho broke in. "Ambushing him is the best opportunity we have."

"Don't you think he's already considered this?" Omega said. "He's not a stupid man. He knows we'll be waiting for him to come back here."

"Except that he thinks we're still behind him. I don't know what would have taken him so long. Maybe he got lost, or maybe the book wasn't where he left it."

They looked at me like I had three heads. "Where else would the book be?"

"I've thought about that," I said. "We didn't find it on the way here and we haven't come across it in the cavern with Sig. So someone else must have found it. Maybe the Cosmonauts followed us, whether to try and get us back, or just to retrieve their book. They could have discovered it and taken it back with them. That could explain why it's taken Reynard so long to get here. He did leave it somewhere along the trek back to the ship, but perhaps when he went back for it he found it was missing."

"So he knows it must now be back here with the Cosmonauts," Rho said, "and he's going to try to get it before we do."

"Either that or he's come back for the Cosmonauts as well," I said. "And if that's the case, we've got bigger problems."

"What should we do, wait for him or get to the Cosmonauts and warn them?" Chi asked.

Rho glanced at Omega, then at me. "I vote we stay here and intercept Reynard. Once we have him we can make our decision."

I agreed with her, but I kept my feelings to myself until I heard what Omega thought we should do. I didn't know what would happen if we ended up at a stalemate.

"Chi?" he said, "what about you?"

"We'd be saving ourselves a lot of trouble if we went to the Cosmonauts and got their advice. After all, they know the layout of this compound and of the planet. We have all of the disadvantages and none of the advantages."

Omega turned to me. "Zeta?"

"I'm with Rho."

"I thought you might be," he said. "That's too bad, because I think the book, Reynard and all the answers lie with the Cosmonauts." He looked at Rho and Chi. "Here's what we're going to do."

As it turned out, Omega decided that Rho and Chi should stay together at the base of the wall near the stairs, while he and I took the tunnel to get to the Cosmonaut's ecosphere. I wondered how they would feel about our return. Betrayed by me? Threatened by having the rest of the recruits here? Or regretting the decision not to put Reynard to death when they had the chance?

I worried about leaving Rho with Chi and the off-chance they'd have to dispatch Reynard. Compassion was Rho's downfall, while Chi's was basic inexperience. Neither would ever have the cunning nor skills of Reynard. They just weren't children of the same era as he. Luck would have to weigh in heavily should they encounter him.

On the long mauve trip down the length of the tunnel, Omega and I scarcely spoke. Did he consider me a bloodthirsty seeker of vengeance that I would wish to capture Reynard in lieu of gaining knowledge about the ancients? Except what he didn't know about me was that what I'd learned while in captivity. I had come to understand both thoughts: War vs peace. Us vs them.

We finally emerged into the terrarium that was the home of the Cosmonauts. Omega's eyes widened in amazement and I heard his sudden intake of breath. All my descriptions of the place hadn't created images in his mind to rival what he saw. The vibrant green foliage cocooned within what could have been a blue-violet sunset, had sun existed here. I heard something I hadn't noticed when I was here before: the sound of insects reminiscent of crickets.

We stood waiting and eventually the three Cosmonauts emerged from their makeshift steel shanty. Their faces, what was left of them, completely inscrutable. Andrei shuffled toward me, rendering it as painful for me to watch his progress as it was for him to make it. Omega ventured a glimpse at me, and I realized that in describing the afflictions of the Cosmonauts, I'd fallen down on that as well.

"Dobro pojalovat domoi," he said. Omega looked at me for guidance, but I just smiled at Andrei. I had my answer: "welcome home." I introduced Omega as the team leader, under Reynard. Andrei gave a short bow and then motioned us toward the center near the hut where we sat on the rush strewn rocks. "Where is the Marine?"

"I don't know, Andrei," I confessed. "I wished I'd realized when we left that he planned to steal the book, or I would have warned you. You know my only goal was to complete our mission and return to earth. I meant you no harm."

"We have it back," Andrei said. "Do not worry yourself further. We will wait here for Captain Reynard to show himself, then we will decide if we should let him live."

Troubled, I ventured a look at Omega, who said, "We need to take him back to earth to go through the proper channels as to whether or not he is punished. It's our job to take him into custody, but not to put him on trial here and be the judge and jury."

Andrei raised his stumped fists. "You are now on Planet A, as you call it. Out here, we make the laws. Only we say whether he lives or dies, or is free to return to earth."

"That's just it," I broke in. "While Reynard and I were here with you, the rest of the team discovered that earth's rotations move five times faster than that of Arianrhod's. The Order of World Leaders said earth had three rotations at most, but if our theories are correct, earth may no longer exist. We could be returning to a

167

dead, uninhabitable planet."

Andrei pondered this for several moments. "Bring in the other Cosmonauts," he said to me, "and let me confer with Omega."

I did as requested, though I wondered why he needed me to play fetch when he could just as easily have called for them. My feeling was that he wanted to speak with Omega alone, to discuss or argue Reynard's fate. For a moment I had a flash of resentment. Omega was part of our team, and as such, did not have complete autonomy in determining the fate of the others. We had arrived together; we would survive or die together.

When I returned with Serenti and Aleksei, Omega's face had taken on a dark look, while Andrei appeared unperturbed. The three of us lowered ourselves to a cross-legged position in a circle and waited for Andrei to speak.

"It appears our young leader here," he addressed Omega, "feels that it is his duty to complete the mission you were sent here to do, and take your Captain Reynard into custody to face whatever fate awaits him back on earth." He waited for this all to sink in then continued. "I think it is advisable to first have a trial here with his peers, and he should be allowed to state his case."

"You don't understand," I interrupted. "Reynard has most of our supplies, the ability to take the ship, although we temporarily disabled it, and with it, all the phosphorous. Not that there's not an unlimited supply here, as well as hydrogen for the weapons. And he has almost all our arms and ammunition. We could never take him alive."

Andrei smiled and the others followed suit, their ghastly rotting teeth and gums nearly making me shudder.

"He won't leave here without our book. When he returns we will be waiting and that meeting and everything else that follows, will be on our terms."

I frowned, thinking hard. He made a point. Reynard had what we wanted, but we had what Reynard wanted more than anything. He would not leave without it, so we had better fortress ourselves and be prepared for a fight.

"Where is the rest of your team?" Aleksei asked.

"We have two members guarding the entrance to the compound, and we have one member left at the ship," Omega said.

The Cosmonauts shared looks of alarm. "There are two entrances to the compound. Reynard may know of both. If so, he could already be near."

I nodded. "We heard the Explorer as we were descending into the compound. It's only a matter of time before he gets here."

Andrei studied me. "Then he will come to us no matter what. I urge you to bring your other teammates in now, before someone gets hurt. We will be safer here if our numbers are greater." Omega rose to leave, but Andrei stopped him with a look fraught with meaning.

"Zeta will bring them here," Aleksei said. "She knows the way and she knows Reynard."

I stared down at the ground, trying not to be angry with Aleksei because he was right. I did know Reynard, but that didn't mean he wouldn't kill me if given the opportunity. Looking up, I saw everyone staring at me as if expecting me to protest. I scrambled to my feet. Giving them all a curt nod and a grim smile, I left the ecosphere.

As I made my way through the tunnel I pondered over why the Cosmonauts seemed reluctant to let Omega leave. Perhaps it was because they hadn't come to know him yet and didn't trust him. Not that they hadn't been able to trust me not to escape. I exited the tunnel and then made my way to the stone stairs where we'd left Chi and Rho. They met me halfway, and to my amazement, Xi followed behind. Reynard was nowhere to be seen.

"What's going on?" I said. "Why is Xi here?"

"We need to talk," Xi said.

I fought to control my fury. "Omega and I left you in charge to protect the ship and if Reynard came back, you were to take him into custody. You have gone against orders. And how did you get here?"

"After you left," she said, looking a little chagrined, "Reynard returned. He's back at the Astraeus."

"What?"

She held up her hand, "Hear me out. While there is the evidence we found earlier that he's been working with Hermes, I think there's more to it than that. Reynard is not what we think he is.

"I managed to restore several deleted messages from the transmission log. Reynard told Hermes about discovering the lost Cosmonauts and their book with instructions for the bomb. Hermes ordered Reynard to bring back the book because for some time now he has been plotting to overthrow the rest of the OWL and take complete power. Our mission and your discovery presented the perfect opportunity. I think that at first Reynard agreed to do what was asked. Then he realized that as bad as living under the conditions imposed by the OWL, living under a dictatorship that would likely result with Hermes as leader would be much worse."

While she spoke I'd been fidgeting in frustration with the question of the day. "That doesn't explain why you're here and Reynard is back at the ship."

"Reynard doubled back from wherever he'd gone to search for the book. He discovered me rifling through his things. I thought you'd all be gone for days, including

Reynard. After the initial yelling at each other to drop our weapons, he managed to overpower me."

Knowing Reynard, this sounded likely. Reynard would have had the element of surprise with her buried deep in his secrets. She wasn't making me any less angry, but I let her continue.

As if unable to make eye contact with anyone, she turned her back to us, bent, and adjusted her boot latches.

"He didn't bother tying me up, just left me sitting there with his pistol pointed at me while he checked to see what I'd discovered in his things. He said that once he'd explained himself he'd set me free to meet up with you and share his plan."

"How did he account for his call to CUB telling them that we were all dead?"

"He said that was when he was still going along with Hermes' directives. I'm convinced he has decided to do the right thing. Or maybe he was only letting Hermes believe what he wanted, that he was working with him all along."

"And what makes you think that?" I couldn't keep the sarcasm from my voice. "Did he manage to convince you with his charming ways?" In the time I'd spent with Reynard I knew that despite his harsh exterior he could be extremely persuasive. What could he have said to Xi to change her mind about him, especially since she held him responsible for Sig's death?

"He wants me to get the book from the Cosmonauts and bring it back to him. When we return to earth Reynard will have both the phosphorous and the book, and in it the instructions for creating a hydrogen bomb. He will then expose Hermes to the rest of the OWL for what he is, and the treason he tried to get Reynard to commit. But if he attempts to communicate with the other members of the OWL from here, telling them that Hermes is a double-crossing traitor, it will be virtually impossible. Hermes is in a position of power right now back on earth, but when Reynard returns he'll be able to present them with the evidence."

"It sounds too slick." I couldn't disguise how dubious I felt about the entire event. "There's something that doesn't smell right. What's to prevent Reynard from doing just the opposite, which is what Hermes wants. Reynard goes back, gives Hermes the book he's been paid to find, and overthrows the other leaders of the OWL."

Xi shook her head. "We really can't know for sure. We either trust Reynard is doing what is right, or just go on as we did before, which is to keep him under arrest and bring everything back and report to the OWL. Then we can let them decide."

"You're forgetting that there may not be an earth," I said. "With the time difference, all Reynard's scheming will be for naught if we return and everything and everyone are dead."

Then a thought came to me. We'd just assumed that Reynard had listened in on our discovery about the time discrepancy between earth and Arianrhod. Was it possible that Reynard, who'd had no opportunity to communicate with Hermes or the Control Unit Base since he'd been our prisoner, did not know about the disparity?

I kicked at an intractable rock. "We'd better take all this information to the Cosmonauts and let them decide what to do. If they don't give us the book, we're screwed because Reynard won't leave without it."

With everyone in apparent agreement, Xi, Rho and Chi followed me back through the tunnel, which I was now becoming extremely familiar with. Together we approached Omega and the Cosmonauts. When he saw Xi,

Omega immediately jumped up. "Why aren't you with the ship?"

I raised my hand. "There apparently are new developments. Reynard has convinced Xi that he's not working with Hermes, only making it appear that way. When we get back to earth he'll inform the other OWL just what it is Hermes has been up to, and they can take care of it from there."

Omega frowned. "What do the rest of you think?" he said, turning to Rho and Chi. "Do we believe Reynard in spite of everything we've seen? Or do we follow my gut instinct that Reynard is fucking us over again and we shouldn't listen to a word he says?"

"There's more," I said.

"Really?" said Omega, eyes wide in mock surprise. "What?"

I turned to the Cosmonauts. "He wants the book. He needs to take it back to prove that Hermes sent him here as part of his plot to overthrow the OWL, not just to collect the planet specimens as we'd all been led to believe."

"Absolutely not!" Omega blurted. "We came back here specifically to return the book to these men. Now they have it we can't ask to give it to someone who wants to use it to destroy our planet."

Andrei spoke up then. "I believe that the book is ours to give to whomever we wish."

"But, Andrei," I implored, "Reynard doesn't want the book to do good, he wants it for evil purposes. Even if what he says is true, the information will never benefit mankind. Only destroy it and the planet. Just as it did in the last war. That's why the OWL banned all weapons of mass destruction and the means to produce them."

"There's something you aren't taking into consideration," Xi said. We all waited, holding our breath, knowing it couldn't be good. "Reynard has control of the ship. If we don't bring the book he will leave anyhow and deal with Hermes when he returns to earth. He can tell him it wasn't here, he could deny the book ever existed, or that the Cosmonauts destroyed it. Or that the..." she glanced at the Cosmonauts and dropped her eyes... "that they're dead."

"Then let him," said Omega. "No one besides Reynard and Hermes wants that information to fall into the wrong hands. It's too dangerous. It's dangerous to us all."

Aleksei smiled. I saw Rho recoil, unused to the sight of his rotted, foul teeth. Out of politeness she recovered her composure.

"I have an idea," Aleksei said, "where everyone can win." He stood with difficulty and moved in the direction of the hut. He was gone for several moments then returned with the book, wrapped up like a Christmas parcel in folds of rush matting.

"Take this to Captain Reynard with the blessing of the Cosmonauts," he said. "Implore that he uses it for only good, and that the right people have it and will understand what to do with it."

"That might work with anyone except Reynard," Omega muttered, shaking his head. "You don't know what this man is like."

Serenti said, "We know his kind. We had many like him in Russia, long before this Order of World Leaders you speak of existed, long before other planets exploded and died. Perhaps in some way they will learn from the mistakes of the past."

It seemed a good idea for the team to rest up before we headed back to the Astraeus. In the extreme likelihood we would never meet again, I sat with Andrei, burning with questions about how they'd survived on Arianrhod for over a century.

"Tell me about the landing of your ship," I said. "Did it break upon impact? Was there no way you could return with it to earth?"

"Enough of the engine and body was damaged that it was beyond our ability to repair it enough to return. Back then, communication beyond a certain point was much more primitive. Our scientists would have had no idea where to begin searching for us."

"We have our suits and our helmets to help us breathe," I persisted, "but once you ran out of the oxygen you brought with you, how did you survive?"

"We began by exposing our uncovered skin to the planet's atmosphere in small stages," he said. "Each day we'd stay out a little longer. But then we noticed changes taking place on our bodies. The longer we stayed out the more our extremities atrophied and decayed. The pain was intense. We would become delirious and hallucinated as if we'd taken LSD. We were terrified at the thought of losing our minds. There were days when we couldn't tell the difference between what was real and what was caused by the hydrogen narcosis. Many times we thought of ending our lives. The rest of the world thought us dead, why prolong the suffering?"

"What changed your minds?"

He passed his hand around to encompass the eco-sphere. "We discovered this cave. When we first found it, there was not much more than a small opening underneath a rock exposed. Someone, Aleksei I think, had tripped and fallen. While this would have knocked the wind out of him he found that as he lay there, he was able to breathe better than he had since we arrived. He called us over and when we bent down, we had the same feeling. Almost euphoric. We recognized that we were getting more oxygen into our lungs. We dug deeper and discovered a small portion of what you see now."

"Was the wall already here?"

Andrei shook his head. "No. Once we found the cave, we started to construct a wall to keep the Aždaha from getting to us. It took decades for the compound to become what you see now. But what else had we to occupy our time than to build what we could with the tools we had? Ancient civilizations have done with much less." He smiled, almost as if to himself. "When we lived we kept hoping, maybe one day a search mission would come. But it never did."

"You could return with us," I said. "Countries and governments changed in the world after you left." I pondered this for a moment. "Although you may not approve of what earth has become."

Andrei shook his head. "We will stay here. We have a purpose on this planet. For what, I don't know, but I believe we are meant to stay here."

I nodded. "I understand." Of course I did. Although the earth I'd left had little attraction for me. Especially once I'd learned its fate. But my promise to Lucian, that I'd return for him, remained uppermost in my thoughts. Whatever it took, I would keep my word so we could have our lifetime together.

XIX

The Cosmonauts fed us a light dinner that consisted of the greens I'd grown accustomed to, scrambled lizard eggs, and the sushi I'd taught them to make by gathering the ingredients and rolling them on a flat surface with their palms. I could see my team was amazed at the food, but I made no mention of the lizard meat in the sushi. Let them enjoy it without reservation.

As there wasn't a day or night, shortly after eating, we said our thanks and goodbyes. Then, armed with the Cosmonauts' precious book, we set out for the ship and Reynard. What our fates were to be once we met up with him, we had no way of anticipating.

There was little to no conversation during the journey. Each of us was lost in private thoughts of how different the outcome of this mission had turned out. Even more disturbing was that we knew nothing of our home planet or its fate.

We approached the ship with great trepidation. Reynard was nowhere to be found on the periphery of the craft. I saw that all our harvesting equipment and supplies were now stowed away in the ship. Before they'd joined us at the ecosphere, the team had readied it for take-off. It was only a matter of time before we'd be taking our sleeping capsules and climbing into our chambers for the long flight back to earth.

Omega pulled the Explorer ATV and the Pup into the ship's hold while the rest of us entered the airlock. I carried the book, keeping it as hidden as possible. I still had my reservations about Reynard's motives and wasn't nearly convinced as Xi seemed to be. But what choice did we have? He was our leader.

When we entered the bridge we found Reynard lounging in a chair at the communications console, one foot tapping on the floor. His expression was guarded, though his eyes seemed to question where he stood with us. I could sense no hostility coming from him, nor a feeling of impending doom. Just the inexplicable calm that exists before a life-changing event is about to take place.

He glanced at Xi first, and she nodded. I held back momentarily before handing over the book, waiting to see what would happen.

"Xi told you," he said, more as a statement than a question.

I nodded. "I'm not happy about it, but I don't know what other choice we have but to go along with your plan. Just know that there are five of us, and only one of you. Once we get back to earth you're on your own, but this time, I want to be the last one into the chamber."

"Agreed," he said, watching me like a bird of prey homing in on its dinner.

"First I want some answers." He frowned at me. "Truthful ones."

"Tell us about the OWL and your involvement with Hermes. And more specifically, why YOU were chosen for this mission.”

He gave a short laugh. “It’s not that exciting. You’re already aware I was recruited by the OWL because of my Marine Corps background and my ability to lead under adverse conditions. We didn’t know what we’d be encountering on this planet. We’d never been this far out of our own galaxy before. Several days before we were to leave, Hermes contacted me and in confidence, shared his plan to challenge the OWL regime. He said that no matter how habitable we discovered Arianrhod to be, his goal was to make earth thrive once more.

“In addition to collecting specimens from the planet, I was to search for phosphorite. He cautioned me to only enlist help from team members who could be trusted.” He nodded toward Omega, who shifted self-consciously in his chair.

“Of course, I was overjoyed to find phosphate rock, but even more amazing was the discovery of a piece of a spacecraft from an earlier mission to Arianrhod.”

“So you already knew about the Cosmonauts!” I glared at him.

Reynard slid out of the chair and stood, crossing his arms in an almost defensive pose. “We had no knowledge as to who or what might have been here before us. When Sig and I were attacked I decided to keep the discovery to myself.”

“So how did Hermes find out about the Cosmonauts’ book?” Chi asked, a tinge of sarcasm in his voice. “It’s not like anyone has known what became of them since they disappeared in the late 1950’s.”

“After Zeta and I escaped from the Cosmonauts’ compound and returned to the Astraeus, I re-engaged the communications system and told Hermes about the book. He was ecstatic to learn of it because just the threat of having plans for a hydrogen bomb would further enhance his plot to overthrow the OWL. But for me, I wanted no part of it and instead, used it as a bargaining chip. He could have earth and the supplies of phosphorous to rebuild, but I," he hesitated. "Or we, could go back to Arianrhod, if you wanted."

We all stared at him, trying to determine if what he'd told us came remotely close to the truth.

"There's something else you should know," he said, his face taking on a grim expression, "Hermes believes that though the Cosmonauts' official position was that they were sent out to orbit space and collect data, another story was that they were really sent out to test a hydrogen bomb."

"I thought they just had the book with the plans," I said. "The space missions back then were so cloaked in secrecy, by both the Russian space program and NASA, that there's no way to prove it one way or the other."

Reynard raised his eyebrows.

"You should know by now that what's written in history books and what is actual fact are often very different things," he said. "We've been told that the ongoing destruction of earth is from nuclear fallout; the failure of crops from a lack of phosphorous. But all we really know is what we hear from the OWL. We are never allowed to question them or we are charged with treason."

"Are you saying that the Cosmonauts detonated a hydrogen bomb?" Omega said incredulously.

Reynard shrugged. "I'm not saying anything. The ecosystem of our planet, along with the supply of phosphorous, was wiped out systematically during nuclear conflicts over the past fifty plus rotations. But it does seem odd that a Russian mission set out to 'orbit' earth would become the keepers of plans for a bomb that could end all life as we know it."

We had two days left to make the Astraeus and ourselves ready for the return trip; two more days of harvesting specimens and phosphorite, which Reynard's revelation had established was at least as important to bring back. The tensions between the team and Reynard had dissipated so now a tentative calm existed, though we agreed to never completely let down our guard. Too much was at stake and to believe Reynard implicitly was to be foolish. And none of us were fools.

Though we tried not to discuss politics, given that one of the World Leaders had attempted almost successfully to corrupt Reynard, the day before we were about to leave we entered into an age-old discussion of 'what was it like when you were a kid?' with Reynard. A weary wistfulness came over him.

"As a Marine I fought for freedom for my country and its people," he said. "After the wars we fought were settled, more or less, the OWL was gradually brought into power. It was so surreptitious we didn't really see it happening before our eyes until they were essentially on their 'thrones.' We had fought for freedom, but after the fallout from the warring countries, the leaders felt the people needed guidance and discipline. And so a communist society was born, though we had always fought against communism."

"We're not allowed to use the word 'communism'," Omega warned.

Reynard nodded. "We're not allowed to use a lot of things. The regime we have now, with the new world order, is not a communist society, it is fascist. We cannot speak any other language other than what the OWL sanctions; we work in jobs created by the OWL. There are no existing visible minorities or ethnicities…"

"Which is a good thing," Omega broke in.

Reynard nodded. "It could be a good thing if it were not controlled and forced upon us. People like Zeta are anomalies and if she were not here on a mission, once she turned twenty-one she would be forced to dye her hair black or shave her head, and have permanent dark contact lenses surgically implanted to conform to their 'standardization' of the population." He looked around at us, his gaze dropping to his hands and sighed heavily. "But you know all this."

He hesitated for a few moments. "What you probably don't know is the truth about your birth. Who you really are."

It was as if a black cloud crossed Omega's brow. Rho sat up, more interested in genealogy than she had been about the history lesson.

"Don't you ever wonder about the recruits? Who your real parents were? Or if you have any siblings?"

Omega's face became even more grim. "Should we even be having this discussion? If the OWL wanted us to know our heritage, we would have been told."

Reynard just laughed. "You're such a sheep, Omega. If they fed you shards of glass you'd eat it."

Omega leapt to his feet and threw a punch to Reynard's jaw that knocked him out of his chair and across the floor. But Reynard, though twice Omega's age, was just as fast and back on his feet in a heartbeat. In two strides he cleared the room and had Omega on his back, his knees pinning Omega's arms at his sides, his fist clamped around his throat.

"Don't you ever touch me again, bitch," he hissed, so quietly I could scarcely hear him. "I'm in control here and I always have been, no matter what you think. So be a nice little sheep, do as you're told, and I might let you live to see the end of this mission. Keep it up with your bullshit and only five of us will be going home. You'll be left massaging the rotting toes of those dying Russians."

With that he tightened his clench on Omega's neck and with one hand lifted him to a standing position. Then he gave him a shove that sent him flying back into a chair. He rubbed his hands together as if dusting them off then turned to the rest of us.

"Now, where were we with my story?" he said, as calm as if the altercation was a distant memory.

For a few moments we sat there stunned, like a room of school children who have seen one of their classmates chastised for misbehavior. Finally, Chi spoke.

"I'd like to know more about us," he admitted. "Even if Omega doesn't want to know the truth."

Reynard settled back in his seat, flexing his arms behind his neck as if he were about to tell us a bedtime story.

"You, and all the other recruits, were developed as test tube babies in an incubator in a laboratory they called a hospital. But it was a laboratory, nonetheless."

"Are you calling us lab rats?" Omega hissed from his corner. "I wouldn't cast stones, Reynard."

Reynard just smiled.

"Who are our mothers, and our fathers, then?" Xi asked. "We're human beings; we at least have that much in common."

"You are the product of eggs harvested from female OWL's over time, and fertilized with a 'sperm shake,' which means that unless your DNA is tested specifically, you're unable to know your true heritage."

"But we were tested," I said. "That was part of the readying process before we were chosen for this mission."

Reynard nodded. "You're right. In addition to your skills, the reason you five," he glanced at Xi, "including Sigma, were selected is because none of you are genetically related. At least not more than four generations back. That's so if you do have a relationship and procreate within your team you're not breeding with your sister or brother, or first cousin."

"That's just sick," Rho said with disgust.

"Sick but safe," Reynard said. "If you are starting a brave new world we wouldn't want it populated with genetic defects caused from inbreeding."

I sat there thinking about what he'd said. Several of my recruit friends had been shortlisted for the mission, but had been culled for various reasons, most of which were never given. Just like my beloved Lucian, who had come so close to accompanying us, only to be told he had a previously undiagnosed heart condition. In fact, I'd been selected once before, but never made the cut until this one. Was that because some of the others were related to this team? Or me? The thought made me intensely sad. Sad, but also curious.

"Once your DNA is tested, it's cross-matched and kept in the OWL's private archives."

"Who are the OWL really?" I asked. "They've only been in power for fifty rotations, give or take. Where did they come from?"

"They were once recruits, like you. But they were recruits considered to be promising children who had been taken from parents. People who had been in military or intelligence service. Each leader was selected from those early recruits. They, too, lacked knowledge of their heritage. Only if they were to study the DNA matches would they know if you were one of their children."

"And how about you, Reynard?" Omega spat. "From what sort of tube did you spring?"

Reynard laughed. "I had a mother and father. I came from a military family, one that had been in service for generations. Sometimes they venture to the outside of the pool for talent." He winked at Rho, who blushed. With that he rose and stretched.

"That's enough bedtime stories," he said. "Time for everyone to have a short rest after we wrap up the packing and readying the ship. Then we'll reconvene here."

I awoke several hours later to the rustling of a couple of the team members moving about. I awakened Rho and together we suited up then went outside the ship to get ready for take-off. Omega was nowhere to be seen. I walked over to Chi.

"Last I saw he was heading off in the Pup ATV to Sector 8. There were containers of phosphorous we hadn't yet loaded." He looked at me and squinted. "You might try radioing him to see when he's headed back." I nodded and moved on. We all knew our jobs. It was unusual for Omega to be out there alone, but after last night I knew he wasn't in a friendly mood and preferred not to be in close quarters with Reynard.

Sector 8 wasn't much of a trek from the ship, although once there the entire operation was out of sight without binoculars. Even so, the planet's dim blue-mauve glow made it virtually impossible to make out anything at a distance other than operating lights. Omega had taken the ATV as carrying the harvested white phosphorous on foot was not an option.

I traced the well-known route, noting the landmark flags we'd placed along so as not to get lost. The thought of losing my way and getting disoriented to the surroundings made me nervous. Communicators were hit-or-miss at the best of times and I realized that although I'd asked Chi about Omega's whereabouts, I hadn't specifically said I was heading out to Sector 8. If anything were to happen, though, I felt confident he'd figure that much out and let the others know where I went.

I reached the harvest zone and immediately located the loaded Explorer, but still no evidence of Omega. This in itself wasn't unusual. He was probably out in a further section, testing before he filled another container. I checked the ATV and saw most of the containers were fully loaded. Omega would not be far away as there wasn't room for much more and still leave space for him to drive.

I was about to leave my tag to let Omega know I'd been there when I heard a sound that stopped me in my tracks. That skittering, scraping of something not human. And I'd heard it before. An Aždaha was nearby. I glanced around, but couldn't see it. Pulling out my communicator I tried to radio in but only got static. Then it came again. And another noise followed it, this one almost scarier because I recognized it as a moan of pain.

"Zeta," I heard Omega whisper. "There's one right behind you. Don't move. It hasn't seen you yet."

I froze, turning my head to check the periphery. I still couldn't see it, nor could I see Omega, even though I realized I must be staring directly toward him as that's where his voice came from.

"Where are you?"

"I'm under an outcropping to the left of you. The Aždaha is behind it. I can't move out because it's waiting for me. It ripped off a section of my uniform and my skin is exposed. I'm not sure how long I can last here."

"I'll go for help," I said. "My communicator isn't sending clearly."

"I don't have enough time," he said. "Do you have your pistol?"

"Yes."

"Then I'll wait until I hear it pull back a bit, then when I'm ready to come out I'm going to slowly count to three. On two, aim, and on three, fire in the direction of my voice, only up a little higher. I'll stay down low, but it will rear up to pounce."

"I don't like this," I said, trying to keep my voice calm, but with both of us so vulnerable it was almost impossible. "My target is too vague. I can't see anything. I'm taking a chance at hitting you."

"I'm going to die anyhow if I'm exposed to this air much longer," he said. "At least this will give us both the chance to get away. If I die, then you can take the Pup and head back as fast as you can to the ship."

Though I could see no shapes in the non-light, I trained my ears to pinpoint where Omega was trapped. The scraping of the lizard as it tried to pry Omega out from underneath the rock was unnerving for me. It must have been torture for him. For what seemed like hours I waited, and then finally I heard Omega begin to count.

On the count of two I took aim and on three I fired blindly toward the sound, aiming straight in front of me. I hear a scream of pain, but it came from the lizard, not from Omega. Where he was I couldn't tell, but I fired again in the same direction, quite certain it was heading for me now. Its footsteps came thudding toward me. It screeched and roared with pain as I fired again. Now, at least, I could make out its shape. And it was enormous.

Taking several cautious steps backwards, this time I aimed between its eyes as I knew its vulnerable spot. It screamed again, then fell thrashing into the rocks, still alive. And angry.

"Omega?" I called out. "Where are you?" But either he was hurt and couldn't reply, or he purposely stayed quiet to not attract the beast. I took a chance. With it flaying about on the ground I took aim, fired and missed. My shot hit a rock and set off a spark. Too late I realized the folly of my mistake. Everywhere around us was flammable hydrogen gas. And Omega had been bringing in white phosphorous, which was volatile under any conditions.

There came a flash and a boom that knocked away all sound, the explosion throwing me high into the air. I came crashing to the ground, instinctively rolling away from the flames and broiling bits of lizard flesh all around me. Boom after boom deafened me. I rolled to my stomach and scrambled away from the fire that spread rapidly across the ground.

No human sounds emerged other than my own groans of pain. I knew Omega must be dead. No one could have survived an explosion of such force that close. I didn't have time to mourn. I managed to roll painfully to a sitting position, then made my way to the ATV and grabbed the inadequate fire retardant. I doused the fires as fast as they sprang up around me, not taking a moment to assess my own injuries. Eventually when I had put them all out I sat back on the ATV and surveyed what I could see.

There was a deep hole where Sector 8 had been. That was where Omega was working. Chunks of lizard lay all over the periphery. I made my way to what remained of Sector 8, trying to remember exactly how it had been before the explosion, but everything now just lay in a pile of dark smoldering rubble. Of Omega there was no sign, and though I saw blood it could easily have belonged to the lizard. I heard yelling from behind me and turned to see Rho and Reynard running toward me.

"Are you all right?" Rho cried as she approached. Tentatively she touched me, unsure of where I might be injured.

"What the hell happened?" said Reynard. "Where's Omega?"

"He was attacked by an Aždaha. He managed to get away but his suit was torn and his helmet off," I moaned. "He told me to take the shot. I hit the thing, but when I went to finish it off the bullet struck a spark and the hydrogen and phosphorous exploded."

Reynard turned to me, furious. "Do you realize what you've done? What you've jeopardized in this mission? Not to mention, you've killed one of the team. When you reach earth you will be charged with murder. And we all know what will happen if you're convicted."

I lost it then and dropped to my knees. "I was trying to save him. I had no choice."

"There's always a choice," Reynard said roughly. "Get up and get back to the ship. There's nothing left here to pack up or clean."

Rho put her arm around me as I sobbed incoherently. Reynard seemed less upset about the loss of Omega than he was about the phosphorous. And the thought of returning to earth now I would be facing charges in Omega's death was terrifying. More terrifying even than the Aždaha. A murder conviction meant being sent to an isolated prison. It made no difference whether you were young and female; murderers were all kept together and damn the consequences.

I loaded what equipment hadn't been decimated onto the ATV, then Rho and I got on and headed back to the ship. Reynard was busy examining the debris for signs confirming Omega's death. At least I wasn't expected to do that. Omega and I hadn't always seen eye to eye or even been friends, but I had no intention of hurting him. In fact, over the past few weeks there had been a glimmer of affection between us. It tore my heart apart to think that if I had just taken more time with my shot that none of this would have happened.

XX

T-90

Time to leave Planet Hell. With the exception of the Cosmonauts I could think of nothing good that had come out of being on this planet. Would we be able to make a difference and save earth? Or had the entire mission been a ruse, a pointless exercise made up by a foursome of autocratic fascists? It made no difference. My fate would be in their hands once I returned. In that I had no choice.

With the communications system working now that Reynard had enabled it, he sent a final message to the Control Unit Base that we were readying the team for our return. Whether anyone received it, we could not say, as no acknowledgement came back. Nevertheless he ordered us to perform all the necessary preparations to enter our chambers, one by one. Each remaining member of the team would check the vital signs of the one entering, until there would only be one left out. And as Reynard and I had agreed, or at least had until the incident with Omega, I would be last.

But moments after Reynard pushed the send button on the transmitter, a look of concern passed over his face. I saw him rapidly push buttons, then hit send again. He glanced around him to see if anyone was watching and noticed me standing there. He beckoned me over.

There was still no corresponding transmission from earth. I could see Reynard becoming increasingly concerned about this.

"Must be the atmospheric conditions, not to mention the fact that we are so far flung into an outreaching galactic system that there are a multitude of factors that could affect it," he mumbled. I knew differently, of course, but I didn't trust him enough to share what I knew.

Though the time difference weighed heavily on me, we prepared ourselves for the journey, each of us taking the tablet that would send us into a catatonic state for the week needed to make the trip.

As Reynard and I had agreed, one by one they entered their chambers: Rho first, then Xi followed by Chi and finally Reynard. But as he reached his chamber he stopped, hesitating a few seconds before he turned.

"What are you doing?" I said, giving him a hard look. He chewed his lip for a second then sat on the edge of his chamber.

"There's something I need to talk to you about. It's about a few of the things that have happened while we were here that I didn't fill you in on." He appeared to be trying to figure out a way to start. I decided to help him out.

"Just spit it out."

"I left out a bit of the story I shared with you about Hermes. It had been my plan all along to return to earth alone. While Omega was alive there would not have been assistance from any of you in MY mission," he squinted at me, "which was not the same as YOURS."

I frowned. "I don't understand."

"As I told you, I'd been recruited by Hermes to obtain the book that contains the recipe for a hydrogen bomb. He was planning on using it to overthrow the rest of the OWL. I betrayed him. After he thought he'd gotten me to agree to his terms I went to the other leaders and told them of his plan. They knew nothing of the Cosmonauts or the existence of such a book. But once I made them aware they realized the dire consequences of the information falling into unscrupulous hands.

"The OWL and I made a plan. They would have to live day to day with the knowledge of what he intended to do and act as if nothing were amiss until I returned with the book. Then we were going to confront him. Without my testimony it would be virtually impossible to dethrone one of the OWL. That's not how they operate. They are untouchable."

I nodded, knowing full well how the OWL worked.

He dropped his head into his hands and for the first time I saw a side of him he'd never shown any of us before. That of humility. A disappointment perhaps, but with who or what? Himself?

His eyes met mine. "And then I made a very hard decision," he said. "It occurred to me that with that book I had no need to hand it over to any of the OWL. Or anyone else. I had the ability, and the materials, to create my own bomb threat. The other members of OWL might not believe me, or believe in the books existence, but Hermes would. He would convince the other leaders that he was innocent and my plan all along had been to overthrow the OWL. No matter whose side I tried to stay on, my own life and future would be in jeopardy."

"Is that when you made the false transmissions?"

He nodded, eyes downcast.

"So what did you decide?"

He stood up and moved away from the chamber. I began to get worried about whether we would finally get launched or if we'd run out of time. I glanced at the countdown to launch time. He saw me checking it and waved his hand in dismissal.

"We're fine," he said, and moved back to the chamber. "I'll tell you what I decided to do. Nothing. I decided to do nothing. I had no confidants among you. Omega was all OWL. There was no way I could get him to side with me. Sig knew what I was up against and supported me, though I knew it ate at him, especially not being able to tell the rest of you. But he was dead. I talked to Xi when you three went back to the Cosmonauts, and got her to understand. She also agreed not to divulge what I'd told her."

I watched him, not knowing what to say. So that was what had disturbed Sig so much, all that espionage that he'd had to keep to himself. I didn't know whether to believe Reynard or if this was just another elaborate ruse on his part. Could we even trust him to get us back to earth?

"I decided to do nothing," he said, "because I began to comprehend that there was some sort of problem with the time sequence. I didn't know what to do about it, whether it was in fact a time rift, or if it were just an error in the computer. But I figured when we returned to earth I'd have my answer."

I stared at him for a few minutes. "Let's get this thing in the air and we'll figure out what we're going to do when we land," I said. "What you're suggesting is nothing more than a coup. Just telling me about it will get me and the rest of the team executed if the OWL finds out we knew and you get caught. I'm not about to tell the others." I pointed toward his chamber. "Get in. What you do with your life is your business, but I've survived too much to die like a monkey in a dehydration pod."

Though his eyes bore angrily into me as he climbed into his chamber, he complied. Finally, I was the only one left not in a compartment. Satisfied that everyone was asleep, I headed for the bridge and prepared the ship for take-off. There was still no acknowledgment from CUB, which I hadn't expected, so I engaged the auto-sequence launch program. Then I went back to the stateroom and climbed into my chamber.

I awoke to find Reynard lifting the hatch from my chamber. Groggy, I climbed out and sat on the edge, taking in my surroundings. Judging by the LED readout of the date clock we should have arrived on earth. The other three were moving about in robotic fashion, retrieving their gear and getting ready to exit the ship once we'd received instructions from Control. Reynard headed to the bridge, and returned only moments later. His face had gone the color of ash.

"We have a problem," he said.

"Haven't we received the 'okay to exit into decontamination' from Control yet?" He stared at me in what seemed to be a complete lack of comprehension.

"I'm not getting feedback from anyone. The touch-down was uneventful. There appears to be nothing wrong except we're still not receiving transmissions."

"Well," I said, feeling a bit frustrated by his apparent inability to take charge, "there's always the emergency exit. We've been briefed for that. It's basically the same as when we landed on Arianrhod. We were on our own there. If we don't receive instructions from Control, or anyone else, then I say we proceed as trained and exit manually." I turned to the others. "Are you with me on this?" They nodded, no one really wanting to take responsibility should we be breaching protocol. But we had apparently been on the ground for at least a half-hour, we should have heard something by now.

Apparently coming out of his fugue, Reynard made for the bridge and set us up for disembarking from the ship. After a few minutes he gave us the 'all ready' signal and we lined up to leave. He pushed the switch, the ship's hatch door retracted, and as we waited for the walkway to descend we were able to view what awaited us on the tarmac.

Which was absolutely nothing. Nothing, that is, except an overpowering heat and the smell of fumes from the ship's cooling thrusters. We stepped outside into burning sunlight, such a vast difference from Arianrhod, and were met with a fierce wind churning clouds of dust into our faces. Shielding my eyes I glanced around, searching for a greeting party. But there was no one in sight. In the distance I could see the Control building and turning to my team I said, "Let's get inside and out of this wind." For a few minutes, Reynard stared around appearing nonplussed, then followed the rest of us.

We walked into the building, certain we would be greeted by staff members frantic that we'd outstepped our bounds by not waiting for direction. But as we walked on we were met with only open rooms and no humans to be seen. The offices looked abandoned, though not before what appeared to have been a frenzied emptying of drawers and removal of valuables. Nothing existed here except a deep layer of untouched dust, and the howling wind outside.

"It's worse than I could ever have imagined, and it

was in ruins when we left." said Chi. He stopped and turned to the rest of us. "Where is everyone?"

Reynard shook his head and just kept walking, searching as he entered room after room, with the rest of us following behind as if he were our mother. Finally when he reached the end of the first floor he stopped and turned to us. "Something happened here, and it's probably why we hadn't heard from Control after our transmissions. There is no Control."

I heard Rho gasp and turned to see her pointing at the wall. "Look at that," she whispered.

We followed the direction she indicated, a large calendar with a photo of the planetary system above. I frowned and glanced at her with a question in my eyes.

She looked back at me, frozen. "Don't you see it?" she said. "The date. Look at the date." And then we did. The date on the calendar was five rotations past the date of when we'd left on our mission. An overwhelming sensation of vertigo overtook me.

I turned to Reynard.

"What does this mean?" He shook his head and ventured toward one of the desks. He wiped the surface with his arm and thumbed through at the papers on the top. Pulling open the desk drawers he rifled through them then slammed them shut. He turned to the filing cabinets that had most of the drawers thrown open, their contents strewn about the floor. He bent down to examine a few of the files and turned away.

Together we walked through the building, examining anything that might provide a clue as to what had transpired here since we left on our mission. Finally we reached the control room where Reynard appeared to have some familiarity with the layout, though the last time I'd seen it the furniture was entirely different. Computer monitors had sat on desks and I'd understood the day to day workings, if not the system. Now everything was as if from another date and time from the future. Except there wasn't a future because there wasn't anyone here.

We headed toward the front of the building, where the main entrance held a security office through which to pass. Then my heart leaped in excitement. A lone figure sat in the vestibule, awaiting visitors that would be required to stop in and pass a security check before being allowed into the building. We all scrambled to the office, with the same questions in mind. Where was everyone? I reached the office first then stopped, frozen in shock. An aged skeleton, dressed in uniform of a style not known to me, kept guard over nothing.

Scarcely glancing at each other, we moved outside the building, the façade now markedly different from the one we had entered over a century ago. It was as dusty and dry out here as it had been on the tarmac. Not a leaf or tree or blade of grass existed, only swirling dust clouds under a relentless sun. Futuristic inoperable automobiles lined the streets, empty, derelict. A few of the vehicles held desiccated skeletons, their bony hands still clenched on the steering mechanisms that looked like the controllers from the video games of my youth.

And suddenly I was reminded of the episode of the monkey, what seemed like eons ago, but was in my time really only several moons. That gruesome scene in which the OWL had shown us what would happen if we were to fail in our mission and not bring back samples of the exoplanet, and with it the opportunity to relocate our people. Though it had not been part of our team's initial mission, I now knew that without phosphorous, earth would have no ability to grow food and all life forms would perish.

And that was what had happened. Except that our mission was not a failure. We had brought back the samples of soil and liquids from Arianrhod as we set out to establish viability for resettlement. Reynard had brought the phosphorous for fertilizer. But it was too late. It was as I had feared. Somehow earth's time was accelerated over that of Planet A's, something the scientists in their haste to send us out had missed.

XXI

In the end, Reynard took charge as had been planned all along. We headed back to the ship for there was nothing to sustain us where we were. Derelict office buildings, shops, restaurants, all deserted and long dead. Petrified skeletons holding vigil where there once had been life. A wild west ghost town in a post-modern apocalyptic society.

A strange notion occurred to me: a longing to see my old compartment, if my personal things were still there. But of course, it would have long been reassigned to another person working with the OWL, who had given us all up for lost. Then I thought of Lucian. I would never be able to find him now. I could only assume he'd perished like everyone else. And the worst of it was that I'd never gotten to say goodbye. Hot tears threatened to spill but I fought them back. The rest of my team moved about like zombies brought back from the dead. Which, in fact, we were.

Once inside the ship we sat in the bridge waiting for someone to make a decision. We had been prepared for life threatening situations on many levels, just not one of this magnitude. Even with the OWL's dire warnings, we had taken that to be the punishment done to us for failure. We hadn't readily understood that this could happen to the entire planet. And we had a difficult time believing that we were the only five life forms left on earth.

"This was an eventuality I had been briefed about," Reynard began, "but like all eventualities, you never really expect them to happen. We have to make decisions about whether to stay here, investigate what might still be out there for us, or move on. Because there are only five of us left, it would be best for us to stay and work together. There really aren't too many options."

"What about the all the specimens and phosphorite we brought back?" Xi asked. "Can we create enough water to be able to sustain life here, grow food, or is it all a useless exercise and we'll inevitably just turn out like those skeletons out there?"

"I've been thinking about that," said Reynard. "But anything we attempt here is going to take time. Growing things is easy. Anyone can throw seeds at the dirt. It's finding a source of safe water that's going to be difficult. The power or fuel to run equipment has long since been destroyed. Hell," he ran his hands through his hair in frustration, "this whole planet has been used up."

I stared at my hands. I'd been thinking about our lives here for a lot longer than just the past few hours. There was nothing much on Planet A, but there was less than nothing here. Other than a limited, or nonexistent supply of water, we had no idea what other dangers might be lurking. Was the place radioactive? Were there survivors? And if so, had they become marauders who jealously guarded their precious resources? Or were people working together in communes, as the OWL would have wanted? I couldn't help wondering if at the end the OWL had still existed, or had been overthrown at the end.

The OWL had sent us out to find evidence of a habitable exoplanet to colonize, but in the end the only thing that was left was us. And we would survive as long as we could. That's what humans did. The word failure had been removed from our vocabulary.

"So," said Reynard. "Here are our choices, however limited. We have a spacecraft, so we can stay or we can leave. We have supplies to last us for a while, at least until we can grow crops from the seeds we have, or find stashes of preserved foods. The military always had decades' worth of canned goods stored away in bunkers in case of such a catastrophe. We can work at finding those, assuming they haven't already been raided. There are seed banks. And there may very well be pockets of survivors somewhere."

"I don't think you're being completely realistic," I said. "We don't know how long these people have been dead or how long this planet has been without water. The calendar we saw showed the last moon and rotation people were here. Why couldn't it be many rotations past that? For all we know, it's 150 rotations into the future, or 200. So, they could very well have depleted all those resources you're talking about a very long time ago."

I could see that I'd touched on something Reynard hadn't considered. He chewed at his lip for a few minutes, lost in thought. I took the opportunity to further state my case.

"The thing is," I said, "we really don't know anything about earth anymore. We did once, but it's as alien to us now as any planet we could land on if we were to turn around and set out again. There really is only one planet we know of that has life and can sustain life. And we were on it."

Reynard shook his head. "We're not going back to Arianrhod. It's absolutely out of the question. Dividing our resources, our manpower, would be suicidal."

"Staying here is suicidal," Rho said quietly. "I think there is something to what Zeta is saying. On Arianrhod we have people who can show us how to stay alive, how to grow things on a virtually uninhabitable planet. There doesn't appear to be anything like that here. We'd be starting from scratch. And for what? To die a miserable, early death?"

Reynard's cheeks had taken on dark red splotches. Even after all that had occurred on Planet A, once back in charge he wasn't used to being defied.

"You're either with me or against me," he said. "I have no intention of leaving earth again in my lifetime. So, if you want to take the ship and return to Planet Hell, be my guest, but I'm staying." He glared at all of us, his eyes lingering on each person's face a few seconds. "Are there any of you who will stay with me or are you going to defect as those Soviets did?"

"They didn't defect," I reminded him. "They were abandoned. Or, more to the point, never rescued. If they have lived as long as they have on Planet A, I'm willing to take the chance and go back. They wanted us to stay. They're tired of having only each other to talk to. There's so much we could teach them; there's probably a wealth of things left here worth taking back to them." I looked at Reynard, feeling sadness creep into my heart. "We don't have any family here. There is only us. For a short while they became family." I turned to the others. "I want to go back. Who's with me?"

Immediately Rho's hand shot up and she moved to my side. I felt her arm slip around my waist and she gave me a hug. Chi looked torn, but eventually his hand went up as well then dropped into his lap. "I'll go with them," he said. We all turned to Xi, knowing she was the wild card.

"I'm going with Zeta," she said. "It's what Sig would have done."

Reynard's face had gone hard as stone. "I feel sorry for you. You will all end up dying. Probably a horrible death," he said. "Your best chance was to stay here with me. Maybe there would even be a possibility you could return there at some time in the future. After all, their time moves exponentially slower than ours." He stopped, and looked around. "But I respect your right to leave and I will do everything in my power to make certain your journey back will be safe and uneventful.

XXII

Because no one knew what resources Reynard would find left here on earth, we divided up the Doomsday kit as equitably as we could. We shared the packets of seeds, tree and plant roots, and every imaginable piece of information for survival techniques. The problem was that a lot of the information was contingent upon the resources being from earth rather than an alien planet. Still, when it came to our survival, we had the Cosmonauts as our mentors.

After sorting through dozens of buildings and rooms that had been ransacked and looted, we finally came upon a series of maps that showed where resources such as public libraries were. Or had been. It was our thought that we would take as much information on as many inventions, the schematics, data, whatever we could find and however much we could store, back to Planet A. Then we could back-engineer and try to locate raw materials to create the smaller of these inventions, if possible. The challenge there lay in the fact that there had been over a century's worth of inventions and innovations since we'd left earth. It was a daunting task, and a difficult one to know where to begin.

We found what appeared to be a major department store and went around collecting and sorting everything we could pick up: cell phones and cameras; computers and televisions; CDs and DVDs. We even picked up a little hydrogen-run portable generator. Not that we could use any of this stuff on Planet A the way it currently existed, but surely the Cosmonauts would be able to figure out how these things worked and extrapolate that knowledge to recreate potential inventions. The practicality of occupying space with worthless garbage dawned on us, so we ended up leaving much of it behind.

Then we collected supplies, like batteries, wires, raw materials from the electronics department. The more information the package had and the bigger the owner's manual, the more valuable it was to us. We didn't know what we could use, but while we were there we might as well take it. So much of it was completely unfamiliar because technology had changed, but was apparent by the sophistication of the items when it stopped completely.

We searched for food but it appeared that anything edible was long gone. Nor was it possible to locate any of the bunkers Reynard thought might still exist. Though Reynard needed supplies, we only required enough to get back to Arianrhod and sustain ourselves for a short time anyhow, as we would join the Cosmonauts in their ecosphere once we arrived.

One essential task was to locate the public library and collect as many technical books as we could safely carry on the ship. When I finally discovered one, my hopes fell. The austere brick building had been transformed to a mountain of rubble, scattered pages from scorched books blowing in the hot wind. I dug through the ruins, finding pieces of books whose future value to us I could only guess at. On a whim, I threw in some novels and books of classic literature as gifts for the Cosmonauts. Unfortunately, anything ethnic had long since been abolished and banished, so no cultural, religious or political sections remained. I couldn't even bring them back a book about their motherland, for those too were gone.

I headed back to the department store where the team had built a pile of useful items near the entrance. Then I heard a loud whoop of excitement. My heart gave a little jump, but as it wasn't a cry of pain or fear, my curiosity got the better of me. I followed the sound and found Chi in a section with a selection of motorized hover scooters. His grin lit up the store.

"These are on clearance because they run on hydrogen," he said. "How awesome is that? Think about how fast we can get away from those fucking Aždaha!" I burst out laughing. It was the first cheerful thought we'd had in months.

I went off to find Rho and Xi, who were examining clothing in a women's section. Our biggest problem was finding a duplicate for our suits and helmets once they wore out. We hadn't uncovered anything at Control headquarters, but maybe we hadn't looked in all the right places. It's not like the suits were items stocked in general department stores.

When I approached, guilty expressions crossed their faces, but I just waved my hand.

"We need clothes, no question there," I said. "Eventually we'll adapt the way the Cosmonauts have done, but in the meantime we have to keep our skin covered at all times when we're not in the suits."

Rho held up a pair of pants and a shirt. "Can you believe the colors they're wearing now?" she said. "All these earth tones. Doesn't anyone have imagination anymore?"

And suddenly we realized that toward the end when the food and means to grow it had started to run out, rationing of a level we'd never experienced must have taken place. We couldn't have imagined the terror of knowing that each day might be your last. What would be the point of brightly colored sundresses or the latest style of shades when there was no water to drink? It was the same horror that third world countries had known during droughts and famines; that America had survived during the dust bowl of the 1930's. Only this one had been worldwide and had taken the lives of everyone on earth. And all because of a miscalculation.

Sobered, we gathered our items into container boxes we found in another department. We saw Reynard far off in a corner, gathering his own supplies to create and sustain his new life here. I admired him for his tenacity and unwillingness to let go of his homeland. But I didn't have his indefatigable hope and ability to overcome insurmountable odds at whatever the cost. Maybe it was because he was of a different generation and he'd known a life that none of us had experienced, or ever would now.

My hopes for finding a liquor store were long dashed as I realized that alcohol was probably one of the first things to go. I know that's how I'd live my last days, if I knew them to be that. Finally oblivious to what was happening in my world; completely anaesthetized at the end. I sighed. Well, if tradition held any rules, no doubt the Cosmonauts had a recipe for fermenting something.

We were, however, desperately in need of two very important things: first aid and medical supplies. And weapons. For whatever reason, the medical equipment remained elusive. Perhaps as they'd died, the people had hoarded all the supplies, or more likely, exhausted them. It was the same with the weapons. We found a gun shop that sold weapons, and though some small firearms remained, the store was completely devoid of ammunition. So we went back to the department store and gathered up as many knives and sharp implements as we could carry.

Finally we were ready to take all our things to the ship and pack it for the return trip. I looked up and saw Reynard waving at me. Hesitating for just a moment, I placed my last armload of supplies in the box and headed over to see what he wanted.

"I'll help you get ready to leave, if you want. There's no reason why I can't help you get the ship prepared, along with all your gear." He looked down at one of the boxes, saw a football, and smiled sadly. "I found something else you might like to have."

He took my arm and moved me to a pile of books he had acquired for himself. "There's a book here on cloning. I also found test tubes, slides and samples in one of the labs back at Control. There are microscopes and all kinds of things." His mouth twisted for a second as he thought about what he'd seen. "The jars with fluids are all destroyed, though there appear to be some embryos worth salvaging."

He stared meaningfully at me. "It's back to the beginning for me; the same is true for you. The Cosmonauts have resources but they're very few. The more technology you can bring them, combine their survival skills and intelligence with the brainpower the four of you possess, and you'll achieve more than many have done over generations."

I nodded. There really wasn't much we could say to each other. Even after all the turmoil we'd been through together I had a grudging respect for him. He'd gotten us home safely, those of us who had been fortunate enough to survive. I tried not to think about Omega and Sig.

"What are you going to do?" I asked. He scratched his head.

"First things first, find a good place to sleep. I'll split whatever food supplies you have left from the ship and start rationing myself so I don't run out. In the meantime, I'll need to get started on finding water. Once I have water I can cultivate a garden of sorts and live off the fastest growing plants to begin with, the longer range ones, like potatoes, later."

He studied me thoughtfully for a moment. "Are you sure you wouldn't like to stay here, talk the others into staying? Earth has the potential to be the new Garden of Eden now." He smiled, almost as if he were speaking only to himself.

"Think of it. No more religion, politics, fighting. Sure there's no food as yet, but that will come. And with what I know and the resources I do have, well…" He didn't have to finish. It was pretty amazing. The only bad part was, if we were the last people on earth, what was the point, really? Would we pair up and produce children? Or would there be fighting among the females for males? The thought boggled my mind.

He helped me load up the things into the back of the Explorer ATV and then we drove it over to where Xi, Rho and Chi were quietly arguing about the necessity of certain items that would be more space wasters than useful. I turned to say goodbye to Reynard and my heart caught in my throat. Though he appeared completely unaware of it, his nose was bleeding.

I reached for a shirt on a rack behind me and said, "You're bleeding. You're probably dehydrated." Then I heard a sniffle and turned.

Rho emitted a short dry hacking cough. "Zeta," she moaned, "I don't feel well." She staggered a few steps, grabbed a rack of clothes to steady herself, then vomited. With it came a spray of blood.

I heard more vomiting and turned to look at Xi. The whites of her eyes were suffused with red blood corpuscles. Chi had his head tilted back trying to stem a vicious nosebleed. I grabbed another handful of T-shirts and passed them around.

"Oh my god," I whispered, "what's happening to us?"

XXIII

Even as I voiced the question I knew the answer. So did the others. It was what we'd been coached to expect from derelict planets. We should have been overcautious when we discovered that everyone on earth was dead. We were suffering from radiation poisoning. All the education I'd received back as far as Madame Curie to understanding how x-rays worked, flooded through my brain. But the most important piece of information I had was that if we stayed here much longer we would die.

"We have to get this stuff into the Astraeus and leave right now," Reynard said. "The entire planet will be radioactive. Nowhere is safe. Cover any exposed areas of your bodies as much as you can and let's get back to the ship immediately." He glanced at me. "Looks like I'm going to be returning with you."

I didn't have much time to think about how that made me feel. When Reynard had said he was staying behind on earth a part of me was saddened. We needed a leader, more guidance than what we'd get from the Cosmonauts. Well, now we had it, but not in the way we'd wanted.

We gathered all our ill-gotten gains together and headed back, some riding on the ATV, some running alongside. When we reached the ship we unloaded the harvested specimens and phosphorous, which we no longer needed as we'd be going back to a hydrogen and phosphorous rich planet. Then we loaded it to the max with our supplies, cramming items into nooks and crannies, leaving only the entrance to the airlock and passageway to the stateroom and bridge.

"We have the decontamination chambers. Use them to wash as much of the radiation off you as you can," I said. "There's not much else we can do. And hurry up. The faster you get the excess off you the better your chances of not suffering from long term effects."

Reynard had disappeared into our stash of medical books and supplies and was rapidly thumbing through them, looking for whatever recommended treatment he could find. He looked up from his reading.

"Prussian Blue," he said. "It's regularly stocked in our emergency supplies. It will reduce the absorption of the radiation in our bodies." He slammed the book closed. "Doesn't seem to have many side effects other than your poop will turn blue."

He went to the first aid station and sorted through the various medications that we always traveled with, pulled out a bottle, checked the dosage and handed us several tablets each.

"Judging from the rapid onset of our symptoms," he said, "I'd say we got hit with a pretty high level of radiation. I'm giving you the maximum dose."

We took our medication, then settled back to wait in the ship until we felt well enough to travel. We played cards to pass the time, though all the while knowing we could not stay here on earth much longer without exposing ourselves to more radioactivity. In a moment of panic I realized that if the team were lying on their backs in their chambers, they could very well drown in their own blood. Chi hadn't been able to staunch the nosebleed and Rho's coughing had increased to the point she had difficulty breathing.

"Wait," I said. They all stopped as abruptly as if I'd blown a whistle. "We can't go like this, we'll die in those chambers, so what's the point of even leaving?"

"What do you propose we do?" Reynard's voice came out as a growl. His lips were a tight line in his dead white face. I knew he'd swallowed a lot of blood while he was bleeding and he probably felt as ill as the rest of us. "We can't stay here. If we don't leave we'll die anyhow. We certainly won't get well here. In case you haven't noticed there aren't any doctors."

I'd been thinking about it and finally said, "I'd like to go back out there, see if there's anyone or anything still alive. Now that I'm aware of the level of radioactivity, I'll wear the protective suit and helmet and be back as soon as I can. The rest of you can stay here. When I get back we should be ready to leave."

"Zeta, no!" Rho cried. "It's suicide." She turned to Reynard. "Reynard, you can stop her. Don't let her go out there again." But Reynard appeared to be giving my suggestion serious consideration.

"I don't think Zeta's plan is a bad one, as long as she takes precautions and is properly armed for whatever might happen." He turned to me. "You need to stay in radio contact with us, not only to keep us informed, but for us to know your whereabouts if we have to come and rescue you." He pulled his gun from his belt. "Take this. It's got a full charge in it. You know how to use it."

I did, and took it from him gladly, along with my own that still had a couple of rounds. My reasons for going out again were not only to search for arms and ammunition, but anything else useful to us in our new existence. I also wanted to know if there were others who might still be alive, Lucian included. The thought of what his life had been like these past five years since I'd been gone haunted me. Had he married? Had children? Had he been witness to the end of the planet? But the most likely place he'd have been would have been the compound. And he wasn't there.

Xi jumped up. "You're not going alone. I'll come with you." Reynard shot a look at me that was heavy with meaning, and one I understood.

"No," I said. "I'm going alone. We're down to a skeleton crew, sorry for the analogy, but it's true. We can't spare any more losses. But if I can bring back more arms or find more information further away from here, then I need the chance to try."

Xi nodded reluctantly, or perhaps she'd just been making a grand gesture. I really didn't want to go back out there so badly myself. I needed to.

"You stay here until the Prussian Blue tablets take effect and you're well enough to travel. Give me the rest of the day," I said. "And if there's no communication or I don't come back, assume I'm dead."

I heard Rho begin to cry softly, which then turned into coughing, but I didn't turn. They helped me suit up, then backed the Pup ATV out to a point where they wouldn't be exposed, and I was on my own.

XXIV

When I exited the space station compound area, I turned the Pup in the opposite direction we'd gone to earlier in the day where we'd found the department store and library. I was hoping to head out into the country where perhaps I might find ingenuity and human nature at its best: people trying to survive. The road leading out was deserted but for stranded vehicles, either abandoned or with the obligatory long decayed skeletal remains at the wheel. After a while it surprised me to find I was no longer shocked by the sight of this.

Hoping to save wear on the ATV, I decided to try the next abandoned vehicle I came upon, though probably the reason for abandonment would be because it was out of fuel. It took three more attempts before I found a truck with a nearly full tank of hydrogen and nothing dead in the cab. The owner had left in such haste the card key was still in the ignition. Congratulating myself on my good fortune, I parked the Pup on the edge of the road, making a note of landmarks so I could locate it again. Then I climbed into the truck and resumed heading out of the city.

Before too long the ransacked buildings melted way and long stretches of dry brown landscape emerged as far as the eye could see. Dead and derelict. No evidence of life anywhere. I wondered how far I should travel, feeling paranoid that not only should the trucks fuel cell need recharging, but that the truck itself might break down. The ATV ran on its own rechargeable system, but it was limited in what it could carry. In addition, I was constantly exposed to the outside air. At least in a closed cab my uniform and helmet weren't absorbing the radiation.

I checked the fuel system for what seemed like the thousandth time. The indicator showed just under half a charge. At this rate, with nothing I passed appearing to hold any possibilities, I pondered the wisdom of moving on. I decided to drive another few miles and if I found nothing of consequence I'd head back. At least I would have tried.

The road bisecting the dust-bowl grey land elevated toward a range of mountains, themselves covered in brittle skeletons of trees long dead. Knowing steep climbs would use up more fuel, I hesitated for a moment, yet something pulled at me. What once had been thriving farms dissipated into the desiccated landscape behind. But then, far off in the distance to my right, a narrow dirt road appeared, leading off around a bend. I slowed and turned up the road, bracing against the bumpy, rutted surface that jounced the truck.

Dead branches that had once drooped with needled fronds scraped like fingernails against the truck roof. I slowed even more as the lane twisted and switched back. And then suddenly the road ended. I braked hard and turned off the engine. Before me was an old log cabin, the wooden surface appearing no different than the trees surrounding it, as if the entire woods were cabins in a varied state of construction. But there was no indication that anything here would be alive.

I climbed out of the truck, not knowing what to be concerned about. We hadn't encountered even so much as a live insect or rodent, let alone a human. As I approached the cabin I saw that even when it had been occupied, it was a poor excuse for a habitat, not much more than a hovel. Chances are it hadn't even been occupied when the nuclear holocaust that had caused the radiation had taken place.

The front door was open so I ventured inside. The floors consisted of a plastic type material long ago worn out and full of holes. Old papers and magazines lay scattered around. A few rusted and broken dishes clustered together on the wooden table. A wood burning stove with its burner lid tops askew. Nothing of any significance. In the next room I saw what must have been used as a bedroom, for filthy blankets lay tousled about a mattress that rested on the floor beside an old iron bed.

Throwing away caution, I pulled away the mattress and looked under the bed. A large wooden box, half-covered in a tarp was underneath. I knelt on the floor and tugged at the box, which was incredibly heavy. Sweating and heaving, I pulled and yanked until it scraped and skidded from underneath in a sudden rush, sending me backwards into the dust.

It didn't look like much. Just an old wooden box. But there were markings on it that seemed familiar. It was an Army weapons case, of a kind from long ago, and the lock on the exterior had already been broken away. I lifted the lid. Inside were half a dozen automatic weapons and hundreds of rounds of ammunition.

A sudden panic burned in my stomach. How had

this treasure trove been missed by anyone, I wondered. But perhaps the radiation had come so quickly, as it had overtaken us, that when the time had come for people to arm themselves, there was no point. There were already dying or dead. I straightened up and considered the weapons. It would take me several trips to the truck to get them all in, but I had room.

With such good fortune as to finding the weapon stash, I headed toward the back of the house, past a makeshift bathroom with only cans for toilets. Luckily for me the last time it had been used was a long time ago. A few ragged items of clothing clogged the hallway. I kicked them out of my way and stepped across. A door was open at the rear and out the back I could see the woods surrounding the cabin. Making certain the floor was intact enough to walk between the rotted boards, I ventured outside and gazed around.

Then I realized that I had not contacted the team since I'd left the ship. I pulled my radio from my utility belt and channeled in.

"Zeta here," I said. "Do you read me?" But when I lifted my finger from the button, only a scratching of static followed. I tried again. "Zeta here, come in Astraeus." No response.

"Fucking pointless," I muttered, refraining from tossing the radio into the trees. Probably just out of range, I thought, realizing I should have called when I was still on the road and not so deep into the petrified forest.

Around the back of the house there was not much more to be seen except for a tall pile of firewood probably used for the stove. As I turned away to head back through the house I heard a noise. Nothing that sent chills up my back or anything like that, just a rustling in the woods. I stopped and listened, but it didn't come again. Curious, I took a few steps toward where the sound seemed to have come from. A narrow dirt path, overgrown with twisted weeds long dead, led further into the woods.

I headed cautiously down the path, all the while peering through the dehydrated trees and into the forest beyond. As my gaze wandered away from my path, I stumbled over something and nearly fell. The bleached skeleton of a deer, its horns still intact, lay at my feet. I stared at it for a moment, noticing that even the skin was gone, only a few dry patches of hair remained on the ground. The decomposed flesh that might have contained maggots had long been devoured or simply dissipated into the thirsty ground.

After my breathing returned to normal, I stopped again, wondering now if the rustling I'd heard had been my imagination. Nothing here had been alive for quite some time.

"Is anyone there?" I called out. The sound came again, this time a little louder. But it was further down the path and I had a bad feeling that I shouldn't venture out any more than I already had.

"Hello?" I cried out, "can you hear me?" And then the sound turned into a low whimpering cry and now it was apparent that it came from behind a stand of trees, some of which had fallen over onto a structure resembling a beaver dam. I glanced around to make certain I would not be ambushed and moved toward the pile.

At first it was difficult to discern what I was looking at. An overwhelming smell of putrefaction rose up and sent me reeling backward. Covering my mouthpiece with my arm I moved closer. The whine came again. When I looked down I saw what was left of a human skeleton.

And beside it was a small emaciated coyote.

I jumped back in alarm, but it was in no condition to attack. Nor did it give any indication that it was afraid of me. Patches of fur had fallen from its coat due to the radiation. As it lay there panting, staring up at me with pleading eyes, blood seeped from its gums. It was near death, and I knew I should leave quickly should it be rabid and bite me, and yet…

I went back into the house and retrieved one of the filthy blankets, then shook it till there was not much dust. Then I went back to look for the coyote. As I approached it whined and rolled over on its back in a submissive gesture. I felt tears burn my eyes. The damned thing probably wouldn't survive the trip to the truck let alone getting it to the ship. And then what? Could we take it to Arianrhod? Would my team even let me? It probably had diseases we hadn't even heard about.

I reached down and folded its tiny body into the blanket and hugged it close to my chest, letting the warmth of my body comfort it. It craned its head out from under the blanket and at first I thought it was going to bite me. But instead it just licked my gloved hand. I sighed and cuddled it closer. At least if it died it would have known there was one thing left on earth that cared whether or not it lived.

XXV

With still a quarter of the hydrogen charge left in the truck I was tempted to keep going further, but for two things: the coyote and the thought that the ATV might somehow vanish before I got back to it. Although this was highly unlikely, I turned around and retraced the road I'd taken back toward the city and ultimately the Astraeus.

The coyote remained quiet, not questioning its new situation or struggling against the blanket. For several miles I forgot it was there as I scanned every abandoned vehicle and deserted house I passed. It occurred to me that the places least likely to have supplies or anything useful to us would be the stores as these would be the first to be looted. My best chances lay with farmhouses where people would resort to living off the land. Assuming the land was still able to be lived off.

I was reluctant to take any other off roads, not knowing what might lay in wait for me, whether animal, vegetable or mineral. Nor could I rely on the truck. It wasn't as if I could stop by a service station should it begin to overheat. Just before I reached city limits I noticed a sign that read "Dairy Collective 137." A collective was how the OWL managed farms and ranches, and each had the same name but a different number assigned. At the time we left earth, there were no more independent farms or manufacturing facilities.

The dairy's buildings consisted of the typical enormous barns for the animals, and a large farmhouse. In the old days this would have been family owned, but now, or at least when I was still here, it served as communal housing for the workers assigned to farm work. One thing you could say for the collectives, they were efficiently run and clean, if not Spartan in their furnishings. The workers also typically stockpiled food and clothing. I decided to have a look at this one and see what might have been left behind.

Although there were a lot of smaller outbuildings and barns, I pulled up to the main farmhouse. The coyote whined a bit when I left, but I just stroked its head and it went back to sleep. I felt for the pistol in my utility belt. It was ready should I need it.

I decided to check out the barns and outbuildings first and then make my way back through the farmhouse. There was virtually nothing worthwhile taking other than a few hand tools like rakes and hoes that would be useful. I grabbed what I could and threw them in the bed of the truck. If the team figured we wouldn't have enough room we could leave them behind.

Then I moved on to the farmhouse. Though we'd learned about the collectives in our education, we recruits had never seen or known anyone from them. It was a life very different to our own, though just as regimented. They lived under harder conditions than ours, with rigid hours to work the fields and tend the animals. Curious as to what I'd find I moved inside and walked through the enormous farm kitchen.

Bearing in mind that we'd be living the rest of our lives on a foreign planet with no opportunity to obtain dishes, I picked up a few plates, utensils and anything for cooking I could find. No linens to be found, though. Apparently everything had been turned into bandages or shrouds as people sickened and died. In any case, they'd be harder to clean and could be laden with diseases.

I moved on to the bedrooms, which consisted of bare rooms with rows of bunks. There were also rows of cabinets with drawers. Nothing fancy, just serviceable. I pulled open the drawers indiscriminately—there was no need to tidy up after myself. A few items of clothing remained, but I eschewed bringing them, instead just rifled behind to see if there were any personal items. I had nearly given up finding anything useful when I noticed one of the drawers sticking out farther than the others.

Attempting to push it back into place, it refused to move any further. Likely there was something that had dropped behind that prevented it from closing. Giving a sharp tug I dragged the entire drawer out to see an old cardboard shoe box stuck behind it. I reached out to pick up the box when without warning something struck my hand hard. I jerked back, dropping the box. A large black snake slithered out across my feet and disappeared behind one of the bunks.

Though my heart thumped loudly against my rib cage, the snake hadn't managed to strike through my protective gloves. Still, I didn't want to cross its path again. I picked up the box and left the room, then moved back to the kitchen and opened it.

Inside the box was a small book, likely someone's diary, and a wallet. Tucked underneath that was a necklace, no not a necklace, a rosary, for it had an unusual cross at the end of the string of beads. And then to my surprise I saw something that made my mouth drop open. A set of Russian nesting dolls. Just like the ones the Cosmonauts had!

I opened the diary and squinted at the curious writing inside, suddenly recognizing it as being written in Russian. I didn't have time to read it, nor would it have been useful to do so. I needed to get back to the ship. Still, I flipped open the wallet to have a look. It was fat with faded photographs of plump women in long skirts and kerchiefs, ancient bridal photos, and a wad of foreign paper currency and coins.

I put everything back in the box and tucked it under my arm to examine more closely later. At the very least it would be a gift for my friends. No doubt the owner had kept this hidden because of its ethnicity and religious icons, which were strictly forbidden for fear of severe punishment by the OWL.

Leaving the farm collective, I made my way back to the truck and climbed in. The coyote hadn't moved since I left. For a moment I feared it was dead, but it wriggled when I put my hand on the blanket and I felt its warmth beneath. So far, so good. I started the truck, noting that I had only an eighth of a fuel charge left, and headed toward the city.

At first it wasn't immediately apparent where I'd left the ATV. Then I saw it where I'd parked, just off to one side of an abandoned vehicle. I chided myself for my silliness. There was nothing out here except for a half-dead coyote and a snake. But you could never be certain and it paid to be cautious.

I moved my loot to the ATV, which could only hold the ammo and about three-quarters of the tools, then I placed the coyote on the seat beside me and started the engine. I was pleased with myself. The day had been quite productive.

Everyone was waiting impatiently for me to arrive when I got back to the ship, standing on the inside area of the airlock. I walked in carrying the coyote, which they weren't able to see swaddled as it was. Then I stepped through the chamber and into the ship's cargo area.

"What's in the blanket?" said Rho. I peeled the blanket back to reveal the coyote that had startled to scramble a bit. She jumped back. "Jesus, Zeta! It's dying and it's probably rabid!"

I hadn't thought of that. I examined it closely, no open wounds, no frothing at the mouth, probably hadn't eaten recently or been bitten by anything because everything else it could have consumed was dead. Scavenging whatever it could find, whether rodent, reptile, or human, had kept it barely alive. It did look pretty mangy, but so would we if we'd been exposed to radiation as long as it had.

"Get it some water, would you?" I turned to Xi, "Bring me one of those Prussian Blue tablets. I'm going to give it a tiny dose. If it dies, it dies. But that's the only thing that might keep it alive."

Reynard had moved forward and anger reddened his face. "That makes every other stupid move you've made look smart," he said. "It's feral and could bite us. Not to mention, it will use up our own precious supplies, and it's probably carrying a dozen different diseases. Get it out of here and let's get ready for launch."

Rho appeared with a bowl of water that she set on the floor at my feet. I placed the coyote down and it lapped at the water as if it hadn't drunk anything in weeks. Which it most likely hadn't. I put myself between it and Reynard.

"If it doesn't go, I don't go," I said. "We've got to retain some of our humanity."

I was glad to see that Rho was no longer coughing and Chi's nose had stopped bleeding. I snuck a glance at Xi and Reynard. All things considered, so far we had survived two death planets rather well.

"You didn't see anything else out there alive?" Reynard said sarcastically, "nothing else that is going to further jeopardize us?"

I smiled sweetly at him. "Nope," I said, "despite what legend has always dictated, there were no cockroaches, rats or attorneys. Well, there was a snake, but I didn't know what we would feed it."

He spun away in disgust. Chi moved forward carrying a crate. "Put the coyote in this and I'll get it some dried protein. Might as well let the condemned have a last good meal."

"What do you think it lived on?" Rho asked, curiously staring down at it.

I thought of the human skeleton I'd found near it and the snake that was in the cabin. It didn't take much imagination to figure out that a scavenger like a coyote would eat whatever it could find, be it snake, or human.

I smiled, grateful for the support, however meager. Suddenly I remembered the weapons and farm tools.

"I found some firearms and ammo in the same place. Looked like an old redneck lived there off the grid. Managed to scavenge a few things for gardening, too."

Rho and Xi headed out to the Pup to unpack it and brought the weapons and tools, which they laid upon the table for inspection.

This, at least, interested Reynard. He looked them over then picked up a shotgun. "What? No blunderbusses? No flintlock pistols? These are so old they might just backfire and kill us."

I shrugged. "I didn't see anyone else out there looking for weapons."

"You're right. Everyone get this stuff packed up and secured. We need to get moving." He squatted in front of the coyote who had made itself quite at home now it had a bellyful of water and astronaut tablets. He felt its stomach. "It's a bitch," he said. His mouth twisted in an ironic smile, then looked up at me and heaved a sigh. "Damn thing's pregnant."

I watched as the others prepared to climb into their chambers. After giving the coyote a miniscule portion of a sleeping tablet, I swaddled it in a blanket and placed it inside Omega's chamber and hooked it to the life supports as best I could because of its size and shape. Reassured once it was snoring softly, I slipped inside my chamber and let Reynard finish up the launch program.

As we began the countdown to lift off, I tried to relax and think of what life was going to be like once we returned to Arianrhod. It was a daunting vision, like camping 'roughing it style' with no accoutrements, and just going into survival mode. But now we had a new wrinkle. We were no longer healthy young astronauts. We had radiation sickness, no hospitals, no doctors, and virtually no medical supplies.

XXVI

Reynard had reset the same coordinates as our planned launch over three moon cycles earlier. If everything went well we'd land close to our earlier site, and not that far from the Cosmonauts. It occurred to me that we'd have to stop calling them moon cycles as there would be no moon or sun in our future. At least as long as we stayed on Planet A. With no resources to explore new worlds, it appeared that would be where we'd live out our days, however many we had left.

I awoke to find Rho lifting the lid of my chamber and the rest of the team awake. Reynard had let the coyote out of its box, which was now defiled with blue feces. I suppressed a laugh. It was only a side effect of the Prussian Blue we'd given it.

Chi saw me smile and said, "What do you think we should call it?"

"Old Blue would be too obvious," Xi commented.

Rho chuckled. "What about 'dog'?" she said. "It's the closest any of us will ever get to having one."

"How are we going to reach the Cosmonauts?" Xi asked. "We have no way of communicating with them."

We all glanced at one another. "We'll just have to drop in unannounced," I said. "Like unemployed cousins who come to visit and stay forever."

We packed the most essential gear onto the larger Explorer ATV and prepared to head out to the Cosmonauts' compound. There was not much we could do for the coyote with the air being not breathable, other than wrap it in one of our oxygen-enhanced suits and hope it didn't freak out and tear the valuable thing apart. It was still too weak to put up a fuss, though, and had become trusting enough in its human captors to accept anything.

I had tucked the shoe box containing all the old relics I'd found into a small opening underneath our main supplies. If Reynard had seen it he would have made me leave it behind. But I had my reasons for taking it from the collective in the first place: I was quite certain this particular offering would be appreciated.

The four of us reached the compound wall, tired and thirsty, thankful we hadn't encountered any Aždaha along the way. We made our way up the arduous switch-backing stone steps, carrying all we could manage of our precious cargo. Mine, useless though it was, consisted of my new friend, "Dog," and the box of relics, which the others were not aware of. It was not an easy journey, made especially difficult when traveling through the tunnel to the ecosphere.

Once we'd reached the top, we descended down the inside and made our way to the entrance to the Cosmonaut's ecosphere. No one had told Xi about the shrine to Sig that existed within these walls. Perhaps one day we would find the way. I also hadn't had the opportunity to check out the other cave I'd seen before. I made a mental note to ask Andrei about it as it would be impossible for them not to know of its existence.

Andrei met us as we approached the center of the compound. At first I hardly recognized him. He walked more upright than I'd ever seen him do before, with a youthful bounce to his step. As I got closer I realized that the skin on his face looked healthier, with a bit of a glow, and his fingers weren't quite so, well, stumpy. He had short black hair growing in like a newborn baby. Even his eyes, which I'd never noticed were blue, appeared clear and healthy. I stared questioningly at him, but he glanced away quickly and as I didn't want to bring attention to his degenerative state, I said nothing.

The Cosmonauts, of course, were not expecting us. Though surprised, they were all heartbreakingly overjoyed to see everyone, including Reynard. I smiled at them in wonderment. Aleksei and Serenti's countenances had also improved, their skin exhibiting a healthier glow as if freshly exfoliated. Their hair, too, was growing in. Aleksei's was a light blonde, and Serenti's a deep auburn. As when we last were here, I noticed a subtle change in all of them. They looked more alive, healthier, than before. I chided myself at the notion that it might be due to the influence of having young women, fairly attractive ones, I thought modestly, in their midst. Would that be enough to rejuvenate 150-year-old men? They glanced around us, as if counting heads.

"Omega?" said Andrei. I shook my head. They hadn't known about the accident. Something for which I would never forgive myself. Andrei got it, nodding sorrowfully. Omega had been as close to a comrade as they had known since they'd left their native Russia over a century ago. Andrei especially, had appeared to grow fond of him in their short time together. With only a handful of humans to connect with, each loss was exponentially worse than it would have been in their previous life. I felt his grief, which was no less than my own, still mourning both Omega and Lucian.

"To what good fortune do we owe this visit?" asked Serenti, "we had thought you would be on your way back to earth now your mission has been completed."

Rho and I glanced at one another, not quite knowing where to begin. Should we say, 'uh, comrades, mind if we bunk down with you for the next 150 rotations or so?'

Instead I told them about the incident with Omega, then went on, "When we were transmitting our departure log we discovered an error that we previously thought was just in the computer. But after investigating, it appears that there is some sort of time rift between earth and Arianrhod. Whether it's because this galaxy is so far from earth or there is a time warp somewhere in the middle is unclear. But it appears that earth's time is five rotations ahead of ours."

Andrei frowned. "Our records aren't perfect, especially because there is no sun here, no seasons, or day or night with which to measure time. We estimate that we left earth on our orbital mission approximately thirty years ago, in 1969. Are you saying that the current date on earth is now is around 2072?"

I nodded. "Possibly even later now." I reached into my backpack, producing some of the transmission printouts with the dates.

He scanned the pages quickly then looked up. "There's no way these could be forgeries?"

I shook my head. "I don't think so. Reynard didn't have the opportunity to tamper with anything. And I'm not sure why it would be to his advantage to do so."

"Do you think he was trying to protect your team from the possibility that earth has been destroyed?"

I thought about this. It had crossed my mind, though whether Reynard had our best interests at heart was doubtful. There was another possibility as well. But I didn't want to voice it at this time. The Cosmonauts didn't know Reynard as I did.

"So it appears you will be staying on this planet." He looked pleased, then frowned. "But this ecosphere cannot sustain so many lives."

I felt my heart sink, wondering what that would mean. There were now eight of us with Reynard, all dependent upon a small ecosphere for water, food and shelter. Five males, three females, all of above average intelligence, but with no means to communicate with outside worlds. And possibly at the mercy of other alien life forms, either on this planet, or from elsewhere. Maybe even earth.

Andrei scrutinized me, perhaps gauging how much he needed to watch my moves. What could they or anyone else do to me now? He stood, moving with the ease of a much younger man. He reached out to take the bundle I still held in my arms. I didn't mean to hesitate, but I did, and tried to hide my aversion. But when I looked closer I saw that his hands had been healing. How could this be? Human flesh, at least damaged to the extent of Andrei, was not capable of regenerating like a gecko growing a new tail.

"What do you have?" Now we were in the ecosphere where oxygen was in ready supply, I peeled back the space suit to reveal the poor mangy coyote. She looked up at Andrei and gave a low growl. He laughed.

"Volk!"

I shook my head. "Coyote." Then I corrected myself.

"Dog, now." He smiled and reached out. To my surprise Dog let him pet her. I glanced around. The rest of the team was busy unloading their supplies in the Cosmonauts' hut and getting ready to head out for another load.

"I have a gift for you." Andrei raised his eyebrows. "Serenti, Aleksei, you come, too," I called.

They shuffled up, curious. I brought out the box and lifted the lid, bringing each treasure out separately: the wallet with the currency and photos, the nesting dolls, the diary.

"You may share or you may choose to keep one each," I said. "I found these in a collective dairy farmhouse. In our time they were illegal to own. They were well hidden for if they had been found it would have gone bad for the owners." I thought about that for a moment. Things had gone badly for the owners anyhow. Everyone was dead.

They accepted the gifts, lovingly stroking them as if they were precious jewels: probably more valuable to them than jewels could ever be. Tears ran freely down their deformed cheeks. One by one they hugged me, their smell less repulsive to me now, either because I was becoming accustomed to it or because their health had improved.

"Now we have gift for you," Aleksei said. "Come." He took my hand in his stumpy one and led me toward the tunnel. Dog followed close at my heels. When we reached the exit I hesitated.

"I need my helmet," I said, and glanced down at Dog. "She can't survive out there either."

He grinned broadly, his rotted shards of teeth exposed. "Come," he repeated.

Down the tunnel we went, and as the oxygen content lessened with every step toward the outer enclosure, my lungs constricted. I panicked. My head throbbed. I tried to turn back knowing I would die in a matter of minutes if I didn't get oxygen. But Aleksei just laughed, and from behind Andrei and Serenti pushed me on.

Then we reached the outer compound and Aleksei moved quickly along the inside periphery. I heard a cry and glanced up to see my teammates walking along the stone steps on the wall.

"Zeta!" Rho shouted, "you need your helmet." She moved toward me, but Andrei held up his hand to stop her. Then he disappeared into a small opening only a short distance from the tunnel to the ecosphere. I ducked and dropped to my knees, following him at a crawl. I recognized this place. It was the other tunnel that I had seen on an earlier visit, but not had a chance to explore.

I heard Dog whining behind me. She had suffered so much already, I knew she must be in terrible distress. Her loyalty to me was the only thing that kept her at my heels. Still, I had to put my trust in Aleksei. I followed him blindly down the jagged surface of this rocky burrow. Down, down we went. Occasionally I tumbled then righted myself. Behind me, Dog whined in pain. And then suddenly we were out in the open. Even with the exertion of traveling on my knees and starting the journey short of breath, I realized I could now breathe easily. I inhaled deeply, the pain behind my eyes subsiding. I looked around.

The variegated shades of green stretched blindingly as far as my eyes could see. This ecosphere was exponentially larger than the one in which the Cosmonauts lived. Off in the distance a small lake gleamed like an azul jewel surrounded by a golden ring of sand. The overhead ceiling of the cave disappeared above me into a reflective blue of the lake. Trees with fronds that resembled palms grew alongside. From somewhere in the distance I thought I heard the call of birds.

I turned to Aleksei. "What is this place? If this has been here all along, why didn't you live here instead of where you are?"

"We discovered it only a few years ago," Aleksei explained. He held up his hands. "As you see, it was difficult to excavate with our bodies in this condition and only rudimentary tools. We thought that if there was one ecosphere on this planet, there might be more. What we didn't know was that this ecosphere was even richer in oxygen than the other. Once we began to visit here our bodies started to regenerate. If you have noticed an improvement it is because we have spent most of our time here since you left."

Serenti smiled broadly. "It is like, what do you call it? A health spa?"

I laughed until my stomach ached. I glanced down at Dog, who was sniffing along the ground and moving toward the lake. I shrugged. What harm could she get into here?

"It's like Eden," I said, still too amazed to take it all in. "It's the bloody Garden of Eden." They smiled, knowing precisely what I meant.

"Andrei," I said. "I've been meaning to ask you. Why did you give the book to Reynard, knowing that he planned to use it for nefarious purposes?"

He shrugged and raised his eyebrows. "You think that is the only book we have?" I frowned, not understanding.

"We have three books," Aleksei explained with a wink. "Only one contains the true instructions for hydrogen bomb. We did not give Reynard that book." I grinned and gave him a hug.

By now the rest of the team had followed us down the tunnel and stood about in amazed delight and wonderment. Xi ran toward the lake with Dog yapping at her heels. Rho danced up to me with sheer joy in her eyes. Chi and Reynard approached more sedately, though I could tell that for the first time in over three moons they felt the same surge of hope I was experiencing.

"This is perfect," Chi murmured. "This is an absolute Valhalla."

Andrei nodded and smiled, though for the first time he seemed reserved rather than exuberant.

"Almost perfect," he said, just as Dog tore by us chasing a tiny three-headed Aždaha.

GLOSSARY

Arianrhod

Arianrhod (Celtic) - Goddess of fertility, rebirth and the weaving of cosmic time and fate. Her nature is contained within her name which means "silver wheel" or "round wheel," suggesting her importance in the cycles of life. Other common spellings of her name are Aranhod and Arianrod.

Aždaja

Aždaja or aždaha, sometimes ala or hala, is different from dragons in that it is pure evil and completely opposite to them in its nature. According to legend, it is a dragon-like monster without reason that usually lives in dark and hostile places, or guards unreachable locations. It is often multi-headed and breathes fire. In Christian mythology, the famous St. George icon is described as 'slaying the aždaja/aždaha', and not a zmaj.

Source:
http://dragonwisdom.wikia.com/wiki/Slavic_dragon

Lost Cosmonauts

In December 1959, an alleged high-ranking Czech Communist leaked information about many purported unofficial space shots. Aleksei Ledovsky was mentioned as being launched inside a converted R-5A rocket.

Pioneering space theoretician Hermann Oberth claimed in 1959 that a pilot had been killed on a sub-orbital ballistic flight from Kapustin Yar in early 1958. He provided no source for the story. In December 1959, the Italian news agency Continentale reported that a series of cosmonaut deaths on suborbital flights had been revealed by a high-ranking Czech communist. Among these were Sergey (or according to some sources Serenti) Shiborin, said to have perished in 1958. No other evidence of Soviet sub-orbital manned flights ever came to light.

In December 1959, an alleged high-ranking Czech communist leaked much information about many of these apparently unofficial launches. Andrei Mitkov was, like Ledovsky, mentioned as being launched inside of an R-5A conversion.

Sources:
http://www.thefullwiki.org/R-5_missile
https://en.wikipedia.org/wiki/Joe_4
http://www.lostcosmonauts.net/
https://en.wikipedia.org/wiki/Lost_Cosmonauts
https://en.wikipedia.org/wiki/Talk%3ALost_Cosmonauts
http://www.thefullwiki.org/Lost_Cosmonauts

Unknown Cosmonauts

Many names have emerged over the years of Cosmonauts who allegedly perished in space, or disappeared suddenly from the scene.

These names come from a wide variety of sources, some more reliable than others. They are offered here without comment nor proof of their true existence.

It is likely, however, that the names of the people whose voice and heartbeat were received by the Judica-Cordiglia brothers may be found among those on the list. Presumed lost in Sub-Orbital Flights:

Aleksei Ledovsky (Late 1957)
Serenti (or Sergey) Shiborin (February 1958)
Andrei Mitkoff (or Mitkov) (January 1959)

Source:
http://www.lostcosmonauts.net/unknown.htm

NGC 604

NGC 604, a region of ionized hydrogen in the Triangulum Galaxy. This festively colorful nebula, called NGC 604, is one of the largest known seething cauldrons of star birth in a nearby galaxy. NGC 604 is similar to familiar star-birth regions in our Milky Way galaxy, such as the Orion Nebula, but it is vastly larger in extent and contains many more recently formed stars.

Phosphorous

"Due to the shocking lack of political debate around the threat of phosphorus scarcity to food security, there is an urgent need to take action now to ensure we will have sufficient phosphorus to feed humanity into the future" – Professor Paul J Crutzen, 1995 Nobel Prize in Chemistry, GPRI Ambassador

Source:
http://phosphorusfutures.net/the-phosphorus-challenge/

ABOUT THE AUTHOR

Leigh Goodison grew up in British Columbia, Canada and moved to the United States in 1992. In addition to *Renascence*, she is the author of *Limboland* and *The Jigsaw Man*, medical thrillers in the St. Augustus Chronicles, *Wild Ones*, a young adult/coming of age novel, the nonfiction handbook *The Horse Trailer Owner's Manual*, and *Goodies from the Great White North*, a recipe book/cooking memoir.

Leigh's short stories, articles, essays and poetry have appeared in dozens of publications across North America. For many years she worked in the medical and legal fields, subject matter that often influences her books. Leigh has owned horses since she was eight-years-old and still has three Arabian mares. Currently she lives in Washington state.

www.leighgoodison.com

www.ingramcontent.com/pod-product-compliance
Lightning Source LLC
Chambersburg PA
CBHW060544190726
48283CB00003B/860